Curvy for Him

The Librarian and the Cop

BY

Annabelle Winters

Copyright Notice

Curvy for Him

The Librarian and the Cop

1

<u>BEATRICE</u>

If you're late once more, you're out!

I lean forward on the steering wheel of my battered, powder-blue Honda, squinting up at the red light and cursing under my breath. Those words are playing back in my head as I count the seconds this light has been red. I swear this traffic light is broken. I'm going to write a letter to the government. If I'm late, it's gonna be the government's fault!

If you're late once more, you're out! Out! Out!

I groan and shake my head as I wonder how it's possible that two different authority figures in my life said the same damned thing to me last week. My boss and my landlord. I show up late to the library once more and I'm fired. I'm late on my rent once more and I'm evicted.

I stare at that red light again as my mind swirls with the maddening scenario that if I'm late to work today, the dominoes will fall, the house of cards that's my life will collapse, the walls will come tumbling down around me. If I get fired today, it means I can't make rent this month.

"So really," I think as I rev the engine of my little blue Honda hatchback, which is getting too small for my big ass, it feels, "I'm like one stop-light away from being unemployed and homeless. Good job, Bea. Great fucking job being an independent modern woman who don't need no man!"

I close my eyes tight as I try to push away the memories of the choices I've made, choices that my friends and family told me were the wrong choices. Well, just one choice, really. The choice to say no.

"No," I'd said to Gary two years ago when he awkwardly went down on one knee and showed me the fake-diamond ring he swore was his grandmother's. "I'm sorry. I can't. The answer is no."

Gary had protested at first. Then he'd argued. Finally he'd gotten angry and called me a fat, stuck-up bitch who was gonna die alone. Wow! It had taken all my patience and self-control to not just go off on him, to tell him the truth about why I'd rather be alone than marry a man I wasn't in love with. But I'd held my tongue and just walked away. Not sure why I spared him. I think it's because I wasn't ready to admit what I want in a man, in a marriage, in a happily every after.

I'm snapped out of my daydream by a loud honk from behind me, and I flick my eyes open wide and see that the light has changed to green and in fact has just moved back to orange, about to cycle back to red once more!

"Oh, shit!" I scream, slamming my foot down on the gas just as the light turns red again. The guy behind me is honking and pounding his palms on the wheel, but I'm gone. Right through the red! Gone, baby!

All I can see is red as I go flying through the intersection, muttering under my breath, feeling the weight of all the crappiness in my life coming down on me: about to get fired, about to get evicted, still hopelessly single after turning down probably the only marriage proposal I'm gonna get. What else could go wrong? Bring it, Universe! Bring it!

I see more red, and I blink as I realize that this time

it's in my rearview mirror. I frown and look up, and the moment I hear the siren, I know that the universe has responded to my challenge and is throwing everything it can at me today. It's gonna take me down in a blaze of glory.

For a moment I wonder if I should just run, lead this cop on a car chase through town, a chase that ends with me driving off a cliff, *Thelma and Louise* style! I'm gonna be late anyway, right? Gonna get fired today. Evicted next week. Oh, and I have a monster zit on my forehead that I swear is an alien baby emerging from my fat face! Yeah, might as well end it all, Bea. You gave life a shot, and it blew up in your face.

I press down on the gas, seriously considering making a run for it. Of course, it only takes me like two seconds to come back to my senses. Am I crazy?! Am I seriously going to run from the police?! I'm supposed to be the smart girl! So why has everything I've done in life turned to shit?

I'm still muttering as I slowly pull over to the side of the road, shaking my head and leaning on the steering wheel as I wait for some paunchy cop to give me a lecture on safety or morality or how I'm endangering the lives of honest, law-abiding, happy citizens by racing my powder-blue Honda hatchback through busy intersections. My eyelids are fluttering as I take deep breaths, still shaking my head as I stare down at myself.

I catch a glimpse of my heavy cleavage as I glance down, and a chill rushes through me as I wonder if . . . if I should . . . if I can . . . if I dare . . . ohmygod, am I insane?! I can't do that!

"Do what?" I mutter through gritted teeth as I lean back and straighten up. It's the middle of summer, and I'm wearing a thin white blouse with a couple of buttons open. I like feeling the warm breeze swirl down my blouse. The air-conditioning in my car is dead (of course!), and I don't want to walk into work all sticky. Obviously I was planning on buttoning up before walking in through the hallowed doors of the Public Library.

But you've got it all on the line now, Bea, I tell myself as the police cruiser glides to a stop behind me, lights still spinning. The cop hasn't stepped out yet. He's probably running my plates through the system. (Yeah, I watch crime shows. What, just 'cos I'm a librarian I'm supposed to have my nose in a book all the time?)

"Screw it," I say, reaching up and carefully pulling at my top just enough so my ample cleavage peeks out like I've got two freshly fluffed pillows stuffed in there. I've always been a big girl. Maybe it's time I used my God-given assets to get me out of a jam.

"Or *into* a jam," I tell myself as my racing mind spins through a million scenarios. What the hell am I doing?! What do I expect is going to happen?! Some chubby cop sees my tits and decides to skip the ticket? What if he's some super-uptight cop and arrests me for offering a bribe?! What if he's some pervy asshole and asks me for a blowjob?! What if it's a lady cop?! What if—

But then my thoughts just stop, because in my rearview I see the cop get out of his car and stand there, hands on his thick belt, dark eyes staring straight ahead. He's tall like a tower, broad like a bridge, with thick black hair that seems a bit long for a cop. He's got dark stubble that matches his brooding eyes.

Shit, he's handsome as hell, and I gasp as I feel a tingle go through me. Then I zoom in on his dark eyes like I can't help it, and I gasp again when I realize he's looking right at my rearview mirror, right back into *my* eyes!

I'm frozen in my seat, my heart pounding so hard I wonder if the radio is tuned to some drums-only station. There are beads of perspiration on my forehead like I'm overheating, and I wonder what the hell is going on. Then one more look into the rearview mirror and I know what's going on.

He's going on, I realize as I see the cop slowly walk towards the car, glancing left and right with the lazy confidence of a man who knows what he's doing, knows what he is, knows what he wants.

2
<u>BRICK</u>

I want her, comes the thought as I look down at the curvy woman looking up at me from this banged-up Honda that's painted powder blue like it's a child's toy.

"This isn't a factory color," I say without thinking as I take in the sight of her cleavage and feel my cock stiffen inside my uniform. It takes all my willpower and focus to not just stare at her boobs from above and pant like a goddamn dog in heat, and it's only when she turns her pretty round face up at me, an expression of fear mixed with confusion plastered all over that I realize what I said.

"Um . . . what?" she stammers, blinking up at me. "Factory color? What does that—"

"The powder blue," I say, feeling the color rush to my face as I realize I'm babbling like a goddamn fool. Thank God I've got a solid tan going so she can't see that I'm blushing like a tongue-tied schoolboy who's just found himself face-to-face with his secret crush and is about to faint. "Honda doesn't make this model in that color."

And God doesn't make enough women in your shape, I think as I glance past her boobs and see her thick thighs spread out on the seat. I can tell she's got solid hips, wide enough for a man like me to get between. Now I want to see her ass, and I almost black out when I realize I'm just staring down at her like I've lost my fucking mind. What the hell, Brick! You're a man of the law. You're a good cop. You've always been decent and respectful with women. Well, mostly.

But hell if I can't stop these images from rolling through me like I'm being possessed. Images of pulling this woman out of her car, pushing her down on the warm hood of her Honda, frisking her up that skirt with my goddamn face, spreading her thighs from behind, spanking that big ass until she—

I'm so hard that I feel my equipment belt move from my throbbing erection, and I know I need to get the hell out of here. I don't know what's come over me. Maybe I worked out too hard this morning and my testosterone is all jacked up. Maybe I shoulda jerked off a couple more times yesterday. Maybe I shoulda banged that drunk chick who came onto me at the bar the other night instead of calling her a taxi.

"Just watch those lights, all right, Ma'am?" I manage to say as I turn away from her window before she sees my hard-on. "You have a nice day."

I take a step toward my car, frowning as I feel like I'm being pulled back to her, to this woman, this curvy creature in her little blue hatchback. I want to look into her big brown eyes again, caress her smooth round cheeks, kiss those big red lips. I want to make her mine, and the thought comes through so clearly that I just grin and shake my head. You've lost it, bro. Yeah, you're a dude and you've fantasized about women your entire life. But this feels different. It's like you just want to take her, claim her, make her yours right here on the street, in broad daylight! Who thinks like that?!

"An animal," I grunt as I stroll back towards my car, trying to walk as casually as possible even though my balls feel tight like they're gonna explode inside my uniform. "Only an animal thinks like that. And you're not an animal. You have self-control, Brick. Your mind rules your body. That's why you took this job, isn't it? To learn discipline. Control. Restraint. You can't let go of yourself, Brick. Don't let go."

"So I can go?" comes her voice from behind me, and it sounds like music being played by a band of giggling cupids.

"Yes," I say, refusing to turn back towards her, refusing to acknowledge that the voice in my head is saying, "No! You can't go! You're mine! *Mine!*"

I sense the hesitation in her, and I grind my teeth as I wait for the sound of her car starting up. Soon she'll be gone, whispers the voice inside me like it's real. Don't let her go. You can't let her go.

I stop before I get to my car, my fists clenching as I fight the need to turn back to her, to say something, anything. But how can I?! I'm an officer of the law. I can't hit on a woman I've pulled over. That would only reinforce the worst stereotypes about cops. I'm not a bad cop. I have to walk away. That's the right choice.

The sound of her engine choking interrupts my moral dilemma, and I raise my head and listen. No. Is this really happening? Is her car seriously not starting?! Is this fate? Destiny? Meant-to-be?

Slowly I turn on my heel, my jaw tightening as I listen to her try the ignition again. This isn't a dead battery, I realize. A jump isn't gonna get her going. She isn't out of gas either. This is straight-up engine failure. This powder-blue Honda needs a tow-truck.

And this curvy outlaw needs a ride.

I know it before she even asks the question, and I stare as she pops open the front door and slowly gets out. She's in a gray business skirt that comes down to her knees, and when I see her strong hourglass shape as she stands there in the sunlight, I know I'm not saying no.

"No," I say, feeling my body fighting my mind in a way that makes me almost sick.

"If I'm late for work again, they're going to fire me," she says, putting her hands on her hips and looking me directly in the eye. I can tell that it's taking some effort, and she's only asking because she's desperate.

"Call an Uber," I say, tightening my jaw and squaring off with her even though I want to pull her into my big body, feel her soft curves against my hard muscle, stroke her hair, kiss her forehead, tell her everything's going to be all right, that Brick's gonna make it all right.

"Can't," she says, glancing into her car and then looking back at me. "May I?" she says, asking permission to get something from her front seat.

I nod, instinctively placing my hand on my gun even though I want to stroke myself as she leans into her car, displaying her gorgeous ass because she just can't hide something that big and beautiful. I almost groan out loud as I see her skirt move up her thighs. I know she isn't doing this on purpose. She isn't teasing me. This curvy goddess just can't contain that body. She's gonna need me to contain her. Whatever the hell that means. Fuck, I'm losing it.

By now I'm almost delirious with arousal, and I have to swallow hard to stop myself from drooling by the time she stands up straight again. She's holding up a flip-phone that looks like it's from the 1980s or some shit. I raise an eyebrow and frown.

"What the hell is that? A museum artifact?" I say.

She shrugs, breaking into a hesitant smile that almost breaks me down into a lump of jelly. Now I can tell that this woman is shy by nature, despite the show of cleavage. Shy but also brave. A strong will. I see it in her, in how she carries herself.

"I don't want to spend my day staring at a phone," she says, shrugging again and holding that ridiculous phone up like it's Exhibit A on *Law and Order*. "I stare at enough screens at work. And I'm not giving up TV at home. So something else had to give."

Something's gotta give, all right, I think as I feel my own smile spreading across my face. I don't want to smile. I've spent years training myself to look like a bad-ass motherfucker when I'm on the job. It helps prevent a perp from trying any shit with me. Not that I'm afraid of getting into some shit with a street thug. In fact I like to do it sometimes, just to keep my edge, to remind myself I can take a hit and give two in return. I'm a beast in a fight, but this chick with her toy-phone and powder-blue Honda is turning me into a goofy schoolboy. Careful, Brick. Be very careful. You're on the job here. This job is important. It's the only thing keeping you together, keeping you in line, keeping you from going off the rails again.

"Then arrest me," she says, her brown eyes wide.

"What?"

"Arrest me. That way they can't fire me from work. I'd have a solid excuse."

I snort. "Getting arrested is a good excuse? Where the hell do you work?"

She laughs. "Public Library."

"Government job. Figures." I shake my head. "No can do, Ma'am. I can't arrest one of our own."

She puts her hands on her hips and widens her eyes at me. "Um, that's favoritism. Corruption. I'll report you to Internal Affairs."

I chuckle when I see her lips quiver as she tries to hold back her smile. "You do watch a lot of TV, don't ya. Especially if you think Internal Affairs is going to take you seriously when you complain about me *not* arresting you."

"OK, then at least give me a ticket so I can show it to my boss," she says. Then she blinks and I see the anxiety ripple through her. "Oh, shit. I won't be able to pay the ticket, of course." She rubs her chin. "Oh! Maybe you don't show up on the court date and then the judge dismisses the ticket and I won't have to pay! Perfect!"

"Perfect for whom?" I say, shaking my head as I wonder how this woman's mind works. She's quick, I'll give her that. Also fucking crazy, if she thinks this is a negotiation. "You want me to be bad at my job so you can get away with being bad at yours?"

Her mouth hangs open in mock indignation. "Did you just say I'm bad at my job? How dare you!"

I shrug, taking a step toward her, my cock leading the way like it's a goddamn homing device. "Well," I growl, inhaling her scent and feeling her essence invade me like a drug. She smells like a flower, I think. And I wanna put my face between her petals.

"Well, what?" she demands, hands still on her wide hips.

It takes me a moment to realize that I'd stopped talking mid-sentence, and when I feel a car zip by us, I remember we're blocking a lane on a busy street. Immediately my sense of duty snaps me back to reality, and I tighten my jaw and look around. What I should do is tell her to call a tow-truck and get this piece of powder-blue junk off the street. But that would cost her a hundred bucks minimum. Plus I'd have to stand here and wait for the truck to arrive, my lights on so traffic sees us.

I rub my eyes and shake my head. Cops give rides to citizens all the time. It's not necessarily a violation. And she *is* a government employee, after all.

"All right," I say, spying an empty lot about thirty yards down the road. "Get in."

Her eyes light up, and she walks to my cruiser, her hips moving in a way that makes me want to drop to my knees and push my face in there. But duty before booty, and I stop her and point at her own car. "No, I mean get into your own car," I say. "Gotta push you off the road."

She stops and glares at me, her hands on her hips again. Fuck, those hips! "I don't have time for that! I'm already going to be late! Can we just—"

I square my jaw and center my shoulders. "Ma'am, I cannot leave this—"

"OK, stop calling me Ma'am," she says. "My name's Bea."

"Bee?" he says. "What kind of a name is that?"

"It's short for Beatrice," she says, squinting and stepping close to me so she can see my badge. I almost growl as I pick up her scent again, that hint of body spray, a splash of perfume, none of which can hide the aroma of the woman in her. Fuck, I want her. She makes me want to be a bad cop. So what if I get fired? I don't need the money anyway. My parents didn't do much in the way of raising me, but they left me a trust fund that makes it so I don't actually need to work.

"Brick?" she says, snorting and then covering her mouth. "You're making fun of my name when your name is *Brick*? What's that short for?"

I feel the blood rise to my face. "Nothing," I say. "Just Brick."

"You're sure it's not Brock that was misspelled?" she says.

"Are you asking me if I know my own fucking name?" I snap, clenching my fists and taking a step toward her.

Her breath catches, but she stands her ground. It surprises me. No one stands their ground when I step up on them. Isn't she scared of me?

"Never mind," she says. "I don't have time for this. Can we just go, please?"

"You know what?" I say, crossing my arms over my chest. "I've changed my mind. I'll call a tow truck for you, and then you're on your own, Bee."

"It's Bea," she says.

"That's what I said."

"No, you didn't. I can tell you're saying Bee and not Bea."

I stare at her like she's fucking insane. "Bee like bumble bee," I say. "That's your name."

"No, Bea like Beatrice," she says. "And did you just imply that I look like a bumble bee? That's body shaming, you know."

I rub my eyes and shake my head. I feel a headache coming on. This woman is scrambling my brain and my body at the same time. "Yes," I mutter, rolling my eyes and sighing. "Clearly you're a bumble bee. Those big antennas are a dead giveaway."

"Firstly the word is antenn*ae*," she says, her lips twitching like she's holding back a smile. "And secondly, bumble bees don't really have big antennae."

I glance down at her big chest like I can't help it, and I close my eyes and wince when I realize she's clearly seen me checking out her tits. Fuck, what if she files a complaint for sexual harassment or some shit? In today's world, just being accused of something like that is enough to get you suspended. And I need this job. Not for the money, but for the discipline it adds to my life.

Another deep breath, and then I turn away and grab my radio. Time to get out of this situation. Would I still be here if I'd pulled over a greasy truck driver with a beard that's got last week's Burger King leftovers in it? Fuck no.

"Dispatch," I say in my stern, walkie-talkie voice. "I need a tow-truck at—"

But I'm distracted by the sound of a door slam, and I realize Bea's gotten into her car and is sitting there waiting. I smile as I cancel the call to Dispatch, and a warm glow of excitement rolls through my hard body as I realize what just happened.

She obeyed.

She took her own sweet time, but she obeyed. This woman is confident, but she's also submissive, and that turns me the fuck on. Maybe it turns me on even more than her wonderfully large boobs and that ass that's built for my big hands to hold onto. Actually, no, I think with a grin as I feel my cock throb like it disagrees with my assessment. That ass still rates as number one.

Beep Beep Beep! I suddenly hear, and I snort with laughter when I realize Bea is honking her horn for me to get a move on. Who is this woman?! I thought librarians were all quiet and shy. Is she always like this?

Only one way to find out, I think, my smile widening as I shake my head in disbelief at what I'm doing. Then with a shrug I stride up to her car, place my big hands on the rear, plant my strong legs firmly in the ground, and push.

Beep, Beep, Beep, comes the sound of her horn again as the car moves as I grunt and push it towards the empty lot down the road.

"OK, lay off the horn!" I shout as my muscles flex and release, the blood firing through my veins as I realize she's playing with me, that she's as excited as I am, that this could be something.

It could *Bea* something, I think as I wonder how the hell she knew I was saying *Bee* and not *Bea*.

"Bea, Bea, Bea," I mutter, trying to figure out if I talk weird or if she just assumed I'm some dumb cop. "Bea, Bea, Bea."

3
__BEA__

Bea, Bea, Bea!

"What the hell are you doing, Bea?" I whisper as I steer my Honda into the empty lot as Brick the cop pushes me and my car like we're toys. I can feel his strength in the way the car is moving, and I know he could push harder, faster, stronger if he wanted.

It takes me a moment to realize I'm trembling with excitement—excitement that I know is more than just the nervous energy that's come from the stress of the shit going on in my life. Or maybe it *is* from the stress. Maybe I've snapped. I mean, this guy was clearly checking me out, and I've been flirting with him in return.

My face goes flush as I realize my panties are damp beneath my skirt, and I tighten my grip on the steering wheel as I swallow hard. Images of Brick taking me face-down on the hood of my car float through my head like it's a dream—a sick, twisted dream. Sex has been the *last* thing on my mind these past few months. Who gives a shit about sex when survival is at stake? When you're close to being homeless and jobless and moneyless. I've been a librarian my entire life after dropping out of college, and the library industry (is that even a thing?) isn't exactly a booming job market.

"Stop honking!" I hear him yell, and I blink and giggle when I realize we've been playing like kids, me honking at him, teasing him for mispronouncing my name. I give him one more honk—a quick thank-you honk as we arrive at the empty lot and I steer my dead-ass car into a spot.

I fling open the door and step out, not sure why I'm so excited. Then I turn to Brick, gasping when I see how his chest is heaving from pushing me and my car in the hot sun. Now I remember why I'm so excited, and I blink and look down, suddenly terrified that if he looks into my eyes he'll see that my imagination is serving up filthy images of his chest heaving as he holds me down and pushes into *me*!

"In the rear," he says, his voice deep and commanding. "That's the only way I'll take you."

I flick my eyes up in shock, wondering if I'm hearing things. "Wait, *what* did you just say to me? Did you *seriously* just say you're going to—" I begin to say before realizing he's walking back towards his cruiser.

"Sorry, what'd you say?" he says, turning his head and raising his voice as a very loud pickup truck drives past us. Now I understand that he meant I need to sit in the backseat of his cruiser, not up front next to him. Must be some rule, I guess.

I frown as I wonder if he even realizes what he said, but one look at his face tells me he didn't. I sigh and shake my head. Maybe Brick is a fitting name. Maybe he's dumb as a brick. No way this is happening. I've always told myself that looks aren't as important to me as what's up there. After all, I know I'm not some supermodel, and I never will be. I know a lot of men will look past me just because of my weight, and so I always swore to myself that I wasn't going to be that shallow when it comes to choosing a man. As long as he's smart and intelligent, I don't care if

he's got a pot-belly or a bald spot or a cock that isn't
ten inches long.

But as I look at Brick from behind, the way he's
walking tall, his shoulders out straight, thick legs and
muscular butt moving in perfect rhythm like his body
is a finely tuned machine, I feel my own body yearn
for his. In that moment I wonder if everything I've
believed about myself, about love, about choosing
a man is wrong. My body's never reacted to a man's
sheer physical presence like this. I've always believed
that love and sex are two different things, that you
can have wonderful, lasting love even without great
sex, that sex is a lower form of pleasure, not on the
same level as true love.

But what if they're the same, I wonder as I watch
Brick get to his cruiser ahead of me and hold open
the rear door like a gentleman. I blink and smile up
at him, feeling his eyes on me as I duck down and get
into his car. I don't even know why I'm even thinking
all this crap. There's nothing happening here. Nothing's *going* to happen here. He's going to drop me off
at work and then drive away. He's not going to ask
me out. I can already tell that would be crossing a line
for him. He's a good cop.

I catch sight of his dark eyes looking at me in the
rearview mirror, and I blink as I feel a chill go through
me. I see something in those eyes. Something hid-
den. Something he's making an effort to hide, trying
hard to bury, a part of him that he's trying to control.
I don't know how I know this, but I do.

"Take a left up here," I say softly, suddenly feeling
nervous and self-conscious. I look down at my blouse,
pulling at it as I hold my legs together and tug at the

bottom of my skirt. That playful vibe is gone, and now I feel weird for kinda-sorta flirting with him. I feel dirty almost, like maybe I was leading this big dumb cop on just to get what I want.

Brick is quiet as he drives, and I wonder if he's thinking the same thing, if he hates me now, thinks I'm a bitch. I know I'm overthinking this whole thing (I *am* a librarian . . .) but I can't help it.

"Brick, listen," I say, blinking three times as I feel a catch in my throat. I can be shy and quiet, but when I do start talking, I like to talk about *everything*. Brick isn't a talker, I can tell. He isn't a thinker either. He's a doer. A man of action.

But Brick doesn't answer, and I lean forward so I can see through the bulletproof partition. Now I realize he's on his police radio. I can't hear much more than some undecipherable babble from a dispatcher, but clearly Brick understands.

He turns and looks sideways at me. I feel the car slowing down, and I frown as I look into his eyes.

"I'm sorry," he says. "I need to let you out here. I have to respond to a call."

My eyes widen, my breath catches, and that sinking feeling in my gut returns with a vengeance. I'm not that far from the library. I can walk the rest of the way. I'll be a couple of minutes late, but I can probably sneak in and get away with it.

I nod, feeling the weirdest thought like this is all wrong, that I can't get out of this car, that I can't walk away from Brick. It feels like my whole life has been leading up to this moment, like every little mishap and screw-up has brought me to the point where I ran a red light today and then my car broke down.

It's like fate has brought me to this point, and now it wants me to make a choice. Do you want this, the universe is asking me. Do you want this, Bea?

Want *what*? I think as I swallow hard and look into Brick's eyes as he pulls over to the side of the road. But he doesn't bring the car to a complete stop, as if he can't stop, won't stop, doesn't want to let me out.

"Unless . . ." he begins to say before blinking and looking away. He shakes his head and goes quiet, the car slowing down until it's barely crawling.

"Unless what?" I say, my heart pounding so loud it feels like a group of drummers have taken up residence behind my boobs.

"Well," he says. "It's just a minor thing a few blocks from here. Security alarm went off for a few seconds before it was disarmed. Security company called us anyway, asked if we could swing by to make sure everything's all right. Probably the owner forgetting to turn off the alarm when they woke up and then opening the door or something. If you want, I could just—"

"OK," I say, the word coming out fast, like I don't want either of us to second guess this. "Let's go."

"You serious?" he says, and the moment I see how his eyes light up, I know that I'm not crazy. Not in that way, at least. He feels it too—whatever this is. This weird pull, like today was meant to be, like we've both been presented with choices that will determine how the rest of our lives will proceed, like we're both making those choices even though it seems insane.

I don't reply, not sure what I'll say. And then Brick grunts, like he's not going to ask again, like he's taking control, making the choice for both of us.

A moment later Brick flicks on his siren and turns on his lights, and then with a roar the police cruiser blasts its way down the street, towards whatever comes next.

4
<u>BRICK</u>

"**W**hat next, you dumbass?" I mutter as I turn off my lights and siren, take a hard left, and pull my cruiser to a silent halt a block away from the house. "You gonna give her a gun and tell her to come inside with you? How stupid can you get?!"

I don't understand why I did what I did, asked her what I asked, slammed on the accelerator when I should have stopped the car and kicked her out. I don't understand it, but hey, there's a lot of things I don't understand. They say your name defines who you are, and I've never been the sharpest tool in the shed. I just do things that feel right. No overthinking. Barely any thinking either. I just . . . *do*. That's who I am. That's *what* I am.

And it's led me here.

I glance back at Bea through the thick bulletproof partition between the seats. Even through the thick glass I can see her clearly. Hell, she's pretty. So damned pretty. She does something to me. She *owns* something in me. And I want her. I want her now. I want her forever.

"Stay here," I say, frowning as I force myself to focus on the job. I'm an on-duty police officer, dammit. This isn't a date. Yeah, this call is gonna turn out to be nothing—in fact, I'll probably get some rude homeowner who yells at me for interrupting his breakfast or something. But still. This is my job. My duty. I can't be distracted by—

"I'll be here," says Bea from the backseat. "Go on. Do

your job, and then take me to work so I can do mine."

I smile, feeling a strange familiarity in the way we're interacting. For a moment it feels like we're a couple on our way to work, with Daddy stopping at the gas station while Mommy waits in the car. I look past her, my eyes misting over as I imagine two baby car seats, one on each side of Bea, one blue, the other pink, with cherub-like babies staring up at their parents. I blink and shake my head, wondering if I'm going insane. Since when did I start fantasizing about having goddamn babies? I'd always told myself I wasn't gonna have kids, that I wasn't fit to be a dad, didn't want to risk turning into *my* dad. But an hour with this woman and I'm imagining knocking her up? Fuck, I really *am* dumb as a brick, aren't I. All balls and no brain.

"Stay here," I say again, exhaling hard when I realize I've been holding my breath.

"Um, you already said that, Officer," Bea teases from the backseat. But then her expression turns serious. "And Brick?"

"Yes?" I say.

"Be careful."

I grin, feeling a warmth go through me. It really felt like she meant it, like she gives a damn, like she cares. About me. Fuck, even my parents didn't give a rat's ass about me. And this woman I've know for an hour looks at me like that and makes me feel like this? I can't walk away from this. I *won't* walk away from this. I'll drop her off at work, and then I'll pick her up in the evening. I'll ask her out. A real date. Dinner and wine and all that shit. Flowers, maybe. Nah, might be too soon for flowers.

I'm walking up to the house, a big goofy grin on

my face as I imagine that date with Bea the librarian. Then suddenly I'm nervous, wondering if I'm too dumb for her. She probably reads more in a week than I've read in my entire life. Reading's never been my thing.

By the time I get to the front door of the house, I've cycled through a hundred different emotions already, that big dumb grin still plastered all over my face. I've already decided this woman is mine, whether she knows it or not. Now it's just the paperwork. I'll do this right, take it slow. She seems like a nice girl. I don't want her to see the real me quite yet. Don't wanna scare her off. After all, your name defines you, and although I might be dumb as a brick, I'm also thick as a brick.

I shake my head as I think back to the last chick that saw me naked. All that crap about women loving big cocks? Yeah, maybe in some cheesy romance novel they do. That insta-love shit that one of the female officers was talking about at the precinct the other day, where the woman swoons and sighs for the hero's massive, throbbing, beast of a cock. That shit doesn't happen in real life. In real life they imagine something that big pushing its way into them and they turn and run away screaming.

My massive beast of a cock throbs inside my pants as if it's listening to every word I say and replying.

"What?" I say, putting my hands on my hips and glancing down at my peaked uniform. I've been hard since the moment I saw Bea, took in the sight of her curves, that amazing cleavage, those thick thighs, strong calves, nice big ass that I can really sink my paws into. "You're saying she can take us?" I grunt and shrug, even though I'm having a conversation with my cock. "Well, she'll have to take us. Because I'm not turning away from this. This is fate, buddy. And you don't turn your back on fate."

I'm shaking my head as my grin breaks wide again. Yeah, I've lost it. Talking to my own cock while standing on someone's doorstep. Without thinking I reach for the doorbell and ring it, and I'm still grinning when the door opens and I'm staring right down the barrel of a Glock .17 handgun, cocked and loaded.

I snap back into focus so fast that I almost black out, and then I feel my throat seize up as I realize I just ignored all my fucking training, violated every damned protocol, just made the biggest mistake of my life. Perhaps the *last* mistake of my life. Did I seriously just stroll up to the front door and ring the bell?! What I *should* have done is come around the side of the house, look through a window to see what was going on in there, if there were any signs of forced entry, any signs of violence. Home invasion is a real thing, and it's dangerous as fuck. In home invasions, the perps usually aren't messing around. In home invasions, the perps go in *planning* to kill everyone in the house.

"Hey Marvin," growls the perp who's got the gun in my face. His eyes are locked in on mine, and his hand is steady. I'm a big guy, but I can move fast as a cat. I can pull a gun from a guy in less than a second. But this mofo knows what he's doing. He's standing just far enough from me that I'll take a faceful of lead before I get to him. I fucked up big, and now I have no choice but to stand down. "Marvin," the guy says again, his gray eyes cold as steel as he stares at me. "This shit just got serious. Like kill-a-cop serious."

I stand stiff as a wall, my arms off to either side, hands in plain view. I didn't even remember to un-button my holster-strap before I rang the doorbell like a dimwit. I'd be shot down before I got my gun out, even if I'm fast as hell diving off to the side of the door and turning this into a shootout. I've got my vest on under my shirt, but this asshole's too close to miss my big head. I'm done for. It's fucking over.

I blink as I feel a strange sadness go through me. I've never been afraid of death. Hell, as a teenag-er I had a goddamn death wish, with all the crap I pulled. It takes me a moment to realize that I'm still not scared of death. This isn't fear rippling through me. It's . . . it's *yearning*. A desperate need to reach for the future that I saw before my eyes, the future I saw in *her* eyes.

Bea.

Bea and me.

Always and forever.

I'm not going to die today, I think as I feel a cold confidence roll through me as I stare back into the gray eyes of the guy who's got me at gunpoint. And then all my training comes back to me, all the years of preparing for a scenario like this.

"What now?" I say, my voice calm but firm. I don't want to challenge this guy, but I do want to push him just a little, force him to make a decision, see if he loses his nerve. From what he said, he knows that killing a cop takes this shit to the next level. You kill a cop and we'll never stop looking for you. You'll never be safe again.

"Please, join us," comes a voice that I assume is Marvin. From his tone I call tell he's in charge here. "I got him, Mug. You go check the perimeter for his partner."

A chill goes through me as I put together the information I'm getting just from this. They're using names, and that's a bad sign. It means they aren't planning to leave any witnesses. They're using terms like perimeter, which could mean they have some training. Maybe military? Also a bad sign. I can match up with any asshole in hand-to-hand combat, but this ups the difficulty level.

But all of that fades away in an instant, because the thought that really makes me tremble is what Marvin said about finding my partner. I don't have a partner—in this town they only send us out in pairs for certain beats. But I do have someone in my car. Someone precious.

I hold my poker face even as I feel my body tense up at the thought of Bea being taken by these goons. I tell myself that I parked on the next block, so maybe Mug will look around and simply assume I came on foot. Then eventually Bea will get tired of waiting, won't she? She'll sense something is wrong. She'll call for help. At the very least, she'll get herself out of there.

Marvin gestures with his head for me to step into the house, and I do it. I think about trying something, rolling the dice that Marvin doesn't score a head shot. A few gunshots will alert the neighbors, and someone will call 911. But then what? There could be more of them inside. They could have a family as hostages. These guys will just shoot everyone else in the house and get the hell out. Not a good ending.

"No black-and-white in sight," Mug reports as I step into the house and quickly survey the scene. Everything looks clean and in place. No signs of violence or struggle. No blood stains on the carpet. Nobody's dead yet. I can feel it. "No sign of anyone else out there either. Maybe he walked here."

"No partner, but he has a car. I see his keys. He'll have parked a block away," says Marvin without turning from me. He glances down at my equipment belt and motions with his head. "Gun, nightstick, TASER, radio, and keys, please." He calls out to Mug as I toss everything onto the coffee table. "Take his keys. Enter from the passenger side front door. Reach in and turn off the dashboard-cam. Then bring the car around back and stash it in the garage."

I close my eyes and bite my lip. Mug takes the keys with a lopsided grin and heads for the back door. All I can do now is hope that Bea sees him coming, senses something's wrong, and either calls for help or gets the fuck out of there.

5
<u>BEA</u>

"**H**ow do I get out of here?!" I gasp, pulling on the door handles of both back doors. I look for the unlock levers, but there aren't any. Then I remember that cop cars are designed so you can't open the back doors from the inside!

I frantically look back through the rear window. I can see the man walking towards me. He's trying to act casual, but he's trying too hard. He's dressed in black, and he's got gloves on. This is a nice neighborhood, and no way this guy is out for a stroll in the middle of summer dressed like that.

"Relax," I say to myself, fumbling in my bag for my flip-phone. With trembling fingers I dial 911 as the man gets closer. I can see that he has a set of keys in his right hand. Brick's keys. I saw Brick take them with him when he left. "Come on. Come on. Come *on*!"

But I hear nothing but a beep from my phone, and I frown and stare at the screen in disbelief.

"No Service," says the phone like it's mocking me.

I move the phone closer to the window, holding it as high as I can, trying to give it a direct line to the sky so it can pick up a satellite signal even though I have no clue how this old phone works. But still no service, and I just scream and fling the phone at the partition in front of me, yelping as it bounces off the bulletproof glass and clocks me right on the forehead!

My head is spinning, and I'm panicking. Freaking

the hell out. I rub my forehead and awkwardly turn on my ass, raising my legs and kicking at the window in some vague hope that I can break the glass and reach for the outside door handle. But all I do is twist my ankle on the thick window glass, and then I'm just a wreck, trembling and whimpering like I'm a trapped kitten about to be slaughtered. I want Brick. I want him now. Why isn't he here?!

The moment I think of Brick I feel a calmness wash over me, and I blink as I feel myself getting back in control. Suddenly I decide it's going to be all right. All of this is part of a plan: Running the red light, getting pulled over by Brick, getting locked in the car, my phone thumbing its nose at me with that "Oops! No Service, honey!" message. Yup, it's part of a big ol' plan. Fate. Destiny. Meant-to-be. Happily ever after.

I feel a smile break on my face, and I decide that I've certifiably gone insane. No one knows how they'll react in a crisis, and clearly I'm one of those who just goes crazy in the weirdest damned way. Maybe my mind has just broken away from reality, which is why I'm smiling and telling myself that this is the beginning of some fated love story and not the end of my miserable little life.

"Well, hello, Darling," comes the man's voice from the front seat, and I swallow hard and watch as he reaches a long, tattooed arm into the car and flips off the dashboard-cam. "You been a bad girl today? Whoring yourself on the streets of our nice town?"

He doesn't wait for an answer, and a few seconds later he's walked around and slipped into the driver's seat. I'm still swallowing hard, breathing deep, that crazy smile still on my face as he slowly pulls the car down the alley and drives into the open garage behind the house. A moment later the garage doors come down, and everything goes dark until the automatic lights flicker on.

A million thoughts bombard me like a hail of bullets as the man pulls open the back door and I step out like I'm in a dream. I'm almost puzzled by how calm I feel. I know it's insane, because I'm probably going to be raped and murdered in a few minutes, but I still feel like this was all meant to happen, that this is Brick's and my story, this is our path to someplace special, that nobody can take this from us so long as we hold on to our faith.

Then I enter the house and I see Brick, standing tall and broad in the center of the room, his ruggedly handsome face twisting in anguish at the sight of me being held at gunpoint. And then that calmness is gone, and I feel the panic grip me from the inside like tentacles, squeezing the breath from me as I blink and stumble.

"Bea," he says, stepping forward and catching me before I fall on my fat face. "It's going to be all right, Bea. I'm going to take care of this. I'm going to take care of you. I'm going to take care of *us*."

I blink as I stare up into his big dark eyes that I swear are glowing with love, like we're in love, have always been in love, will always be in love. There are two guns pointed at us, but I feel invincible, like I'm protected by a cloak of pure magic, protected by the shield of unbreakable fate, protected by what I'm sure is our destiny, our forever.

Protected by him, I think as I hold on to Brick's thick arms, feel his hard body against my soft curves, inhale his masculine musk which calms me down like a drug. I look up into his eyes again and the world melts away, making me believe that everything happening around us is just an illusion, all make-believe, just background to our story, the oldest story in the library of man and woman:

The story of love.

And then, as if to prove my madness true, as if to certify that I'm hallucinating, to verify that I'm seeing things that can't possibly be real, Brick kisses me. He slides his arms around my waist, pulls me against his body so hard I gasp, leans down from his towering height and just kisses me! Hard, on the lips, with authority that I know comes from the stars above, the earth below, the sun and the moon and everything in between.

He kisses me.

By God, he kisses me.

6
<u>BRICK</u>

I hear the clicks of guns being cocked, the voices of Marvin and Mug in the background. But it's all just background noise. It doesn't matter. I'm lost in the moment, lost in this woman, lost in this kiss.

The feeling of her soft curves against my body makes me groan out loud, and I swear I feel her contours fit perfectly against my ridges of muscle like we were designed as a pair, built to fit with each other. I ain't never been the spiritual sort, but fuck, this woman is making me believe . . . believe in something.

I break from the kiss, its power still possessing me. I feel like Bea's kiss has turned me into a superhero, and I almost leap at these two dickheads with my new superpowers. Surely the bullets will bounce off me. They've taken my gun, but I don't need a gun. I'll crack their skulls wide open with my goddamn knuckles! Rip their throats out with my hands! Eat their goddamn hearts like a beast of the jungle!

"Brick," comes her voice from behind me, and I blink as I realize I'm standing in front of Bea, my shoulders squared, my chest and arms spread wide in a protective stance. "Don't be a fool."

My head swirls as I feel anger rise up in me so fast I swear the world turns red. But Bea is right, and I force myself to take deep breaths, circular breathing using my diaphragm, just like they teach you in training. Slowly I calm down and nod, holding my position in front of Bea. My focus returns, and I see the guns still pointing at me. Mug and Marvin look like they can't believe what just happened, which is probably why I'm still alive.

"Un-fucking-believable," says Marvin, shaking his head slowly even though his gun-hand stays steady. "What have we here? A cop and his woman?"

"His whore," sneers Mug. "She was in the back-seat, Marv."

"Say that one more time," I growl at Marvin, that anger rising up in me again, the world turning that shade of red again. "Go on, asshole. Just one more time."

"And you'll do what?" snaps Mug, his gray eyes locking in on mine.

"You won't shoot," I growl. "Neither of you will. One gunshot, and it's game over for you guys. You know that. I know that. And Marvin knows that."

Mug takes a step closer to me, and for the first time I see his hand shake. This guy might crack if I push him. Good to know.

"Stand down, Mug," says Marvin, his tone low and commanding. Now I'm sure this guy is ex-military. "Not yet." He glances at me and nods. "Down in the basement, both of you. Slowly. Do what I say, and maybe you two will walk out of here."

I know he's lying, but I also know I need to buy some time. I was sent here by Central Dispatch, and if I don't call back in soon, they'll follow up. When I don't respond, they'll check my dashboard cam and see that it's been turned off. Then they'll check the on-board GPS and see that my last location was right outside this house. I figure we've got less than thirty minutes before backup arrives. I also figure this guy Marvin knows that.

I glance over at the stairs leading to the basement, and then I shake my head. I'm not going down there. We go down there, we aren't coming back up. Think, Brick. Fucking *think*! Use the information you have. What do you know so far?

I frown as I realize that I do know something. It's not what I saw. It's what I *didn't* see. The house looked spotless when I walked in. No food on the table. No depressions on the couch where the family might have been sitting. No smell of fresh coffee or flapjacks or breakfast sausage from the kitchen.

"There's no one else here," I blurt out as the realization hits me. "This isn't a home invasion. It's just a burglary!"

I see Marvin flinch, and I think maybe I'm not that dumb after all. Suddenly I know I've got the upper hand, even though there are two guns pointed at me. These guys are capable of murder, but they didn't come in here planning to kill. That makes a difference. That gives me a shot. It gives *us* a shot.

"Correction," says Marvin, quickly regaining his cold, deadpan look. "This *was* a burglary. It's now a hostage situation. Basement, both of you. Now."

"Brick, let's just—" Bea starts to say from behind me.

"No," I say, reaching my arm back and placing it on her side. Just touching her does something to me, and I blink and swallow hard, keeping my eyes on Marvin. "All right, listen," I start to say to him, feeling my confidence come back as if just being connected to Bea is making me all-powerful, all-knowing, in control of the world and everyone in it. "Here's what we're gonna do. We're going to—"

But I'm interrupted by the sound of the front door opening, and I whip around and stare in horror. And it truly is a horrible sight, like it's the universe flipping me off, reminding me that I'm not in control at all.

"Fuck me," I groan as I stare at the stunned family of four standing in the doorway, their eyes wide, mouths hanging open, arms full of crap from some beach vacation, all of them gaping at the surreal scene playing out in their living room.

I don't even need to look at Marvin to know that he understands the game has changed. And then I feel a wave of despair wash over me as Mug and Marvin usher the parents and kids into the living room and sit them down on the couch. The parents are just staring blankly at the guns like they're in a trance. The kids—one boy and one girl—are trembling as they look at the guns and then at their parents like they're looking for some assurance that this is just a game, make-believe or something. The parents are in shock, I can tell. Maybe they're jet-lagged or something. Maybe this is just how they're reacting to the crisis—by shutting the fuck down. Still, it pisses me off. These parents should be pulling their kids close, not staring blankly like it's someone else's job to protect their children! Reminds me of my own loser parents, I think as anger whips through me.

I'm about to say something to the children, but just then the kids turn to me and Bea, their innocent eyes focusing on us. I cock my head as I'm reminded of that vision of having babies with Bea. Didn't I see a boy and a girl in that strange fantasy that felt like a glimpse into the future, into my future, *our* future?

"Well, this makes things a bit easier," Marvin says with a grin, but there's an edge to his voice that worries me. "We don't need to break into the safe anymore. Man of the house can just open it for us."

"Safe?" says the so-called man of the house, the first words he's spoken. Immediately I hate the fucker. The mention of money is what gets this guy to focus? What kind of a man is he? What kind of a father? "There's no money in there."

"No money in the safe. Right," says Mug with a snort. "What are we, morons? Where's all the dirty money you made selling out our military? We know you ain't paying taxes on that shit."

The man pushes his glasses up his nose and scratches his bald head. I see a smugness settle on his face, and my breath catches as I feel my disdain for this guy rise. "Maybe you are morons if you think anything I did was illegal. I'm a defense contractor. My company provides services to the U.S. Department of Defense, and we get paid for those services. Now, if you've got a complaint against the government, you can simply—"

"Cut his tongue off, Mug," says Marvin. "He doesn't need it to open the safe."

Mr. Glasses almost falls off the couch, he gets up so fast. A moment later he's heading upstairs with Mug, presumably to the safe. I don't give a rat's ass about this guy. I'm still standing in front of Bea, my attention on the kids. Bea and the kids. If I can get them out of this situation alive, I'll have done my duty. Nothing else matters right now. It sounds like these guys are ex-military, and yeah, I've heard about how the military has been using private contractors overseas. Maybe these guys feel shortchanged. Maybe they're disgruntled about something, feel like they're owed something. That's their problem. My only problem is Bea and these kids.

"He's right, Marv," comes Mug's voice from the stairs. A moment later Mr. Glasses stumbles back down to the living room at gunpoint, Mug behind him. "A few hundred dollars in cash, but the rest is just documents. Useless shit."

"I told you," says Mr. Glasses smugly. Clearly he doesn't understand how serious this situation is. Maybe he's seen too many Hollywood movies where the cavalry always arrives in time. Real life doesn't work that way. "We've got about a thousand more in cash laying about. And you can take the TV and stereo. And our phones."

"Honey, no! I need my iPhone," says the wife, and I almost choke in shock that this woman is seriously more protective about her fucking iPhone than her goddamn children! "Just write them a check!"

Marvin laughs, rubbing his forehead and wincing. I'm seeing some cracks in this guy's cold control. He's not all there. Something's broken in him. Takes one to know one. "Yeah, write us a check. We'll go right to the bank and deposit it. What am I, an idiot?" He turns to Mug again. "Thought I told you to cut his tongue off." Marvin looks at me, then at his watch, his face hardening. "Never mind, I'm just messing with ya. Too much blood. We don't got much time to play, anyway. Cop's backup will be here soon. No more time." He takes a breath, his eyes going cold again. Now I know he's made a decision, and it's time I make a decision.

"I'll give you time," I say, slowly raising my left hand and pointing to my radio. "Let me call in. No one's gonna show up if I call in and give the all clear. I'll give you time."

Marvin frowns as he turns to me, his eyes narrowed like he's wondering if I'm playing him. I *am* playing him, but I'm serious about calling in the all-clear. That's the safest thing to do, in my opinion. Having this place surrounded by cops, FBI, and the goddamn media is almost guaranteed to end in a bloodbath. I got Bea into this by being dumb as a brick, and it's up to me to get her out.

Finally Marvin nods and motions with his gun, indicating that if I screw him over, I'm taking the first bullet. I nod back, take a breath, and then call in the all-clear. My voice is calm and steady, almost casual. Done. We're on our own now. It's up to me. Bea and the kids, Brick. That's all that matters here. Do your fucking job. Protect your woman.

My woman, comes the thought as I blink at how I've straight up assumed that Bea is mine. *Mine*! Shit, I just pulled this chick over for running a red an hour ago, and now I'm ready to die for her?! Kill for her? Love her?

Love her?

I can hear Marvin saying something to Mr. Glasses again, and Glasses responds like he's arguing. But my mind is on Bea now, the memory of that kiss almost making me smile. I want to kiss her again, I think, turning my head sideways so I can get a glimpse of her pretty face. I don't care if I die today so long as I can kiss her again first, make her mine before I go.

"All my money is tied up in long-term investments," Glasses is saying, shaking his head like he's in a negotiation. Clearly Marvin has moved on to getting Glasses to withdraw cash from his accounts and hand it over. "The rest is in a college fund for my kids."

"Yeah, well, you argue any more and your kids won't need a college fund," Marvin growls, pointing his gun at the petrified little girl.

I almost leap at Marvin—and in fact I would have if Bea hadn't silently touched my arm from behind me, like she could sense that I wasn't going to stand here and watch some asshole threaten a child, that I would die to protect the kid even if her father wouldn't.

"Hey. Over here, Marvin. Listen, you can have *my* college fund," I say, the words coming out so fast I don't even remember thinking about it. All I care about is getting Marvin's attention off the little girl. I snort and shrug. "Was always too dumb to get into college, so the money's just sitting there. Barely even made it through high school."

Marvin turns and frowns at me. "*Your* college fund? You're a street cop, man! What do you have in the bank? Like three hundred bucks and change? Shut the fuck up."

My mind races as I scan the room. I see a laptop computer on the dining table just past the living room, and I nod toward it. "I'll prove it. May I?" My tone is commanding, but I'm still courteous. There's a part of me that wants to just let go and unleash on these assholes, but I know I have to stay in control.

"Yeah, all right," says Marvin, nodding as if he sees the sincerity in my expression.

I walk over to the laptop and flip it open. A password screen pops up, and I freeze. Shit. I blink and turn toward Mr. Glasses. "Type in your password," I say to him.

"It's my wife's computer," says Glasses. "Honey, give him your password."

"Cupcake69," says his wife after moving her lips silently for a moment like she's in shock. "Cup . . . cupcake."

I stare and take a breath, turning back to the laptop and looking down at my fingers. My hands are shaking. I can hold a gun steady as a rock, hit a moving target from across a football field. But typing in the word Cupcake? Now that's a challenge for a dumb fuck named Brick.

I lick my lips and stare down at the keyboard. All the letters are swirling around like it's alphabet soup. I thought I'd beaten this shit, but clearly I haven't. Reading and writing has always been a problem for me. It's the reason I barely made it through school, just about got through the police exam, chose to work a physical job. I'm a man of action, not letters.

"Where's the fucking C?" I mutter, blinking as I feel beads of sweat on my forehead. I type something and hit Enter, but I just get that beep that reminds me I'm stupid. Now it's like the computer is laughing at me, everyone is laughing at me, the fucking world is pointing at Brick and saying "What a dumb piece of—"

And then I feel her come up behind me. Bea. My woman. She steps softly behind me, leans past me so close I smell her scent, feel her skin brush against mine, experience a calm like I've never had in my life.

"I got you," she whispers, and I'm almost shattered as I sense the understanding in her voice, the compassion in her tone, the love in how she speaks to me. "I got you, Brick."

And somehow I know that even though she said "I got you," what she's really saying is "I love you." I know it. I feel it. I want it.

I look at her pretty face, all serious and tensed up but still somehow soft and peaceful. I know she was scared, but I also see a strength in her. Again I experience that strange feeling of the world around us falling away like it's an illusion, like she and I are the only things that are real, that this is about us and nothing else.

"There," she says softly, her fingers flying over the keyboard. "Now tell me where to go."

I tell her my bank's name and username, and she's there in a second. Then she looks at me with a raised eyebrow. "What's your password?" she says.

Color rushes to my face as I take a breath. Now she's gonna know for sure I'm stupid. No way some smart librarian is gonna want something to do with a dimwit like me.

"I can do it," I say, reaching for the keyboard. But the letters are still swirling, dancing all over the place, moving like they used to when I was a kid.

"Just tell me," she says. "I won't judge you. Just tell me."

I take a breath and nod. "XXXXX," I say in a whisper.

She turns to me, her head cocked slightly. I see the tenderness in her gaze, and I love her for it. It isn't pity, I know. Pity just makes me angry. Nope, it's not pity. It's understanding. It's acceptance. It's . . . it's love. I know it.

It's love.

7
<u>BEA</u>

OMG I love him, I think as I see the vulnerability in Brick's dark eyes, feel the relief go through his massive, hard, uniformed body as I type for him. Immediately I understand that this beast of a man is dyslexic, and I almost get teary-eyed when I realize that it's possible no one ever told him, no one ever cared enough to diagnose him as having a learning disability. He probably grew up thinking he was stupid for not learning as fast as the other kids. Nowadays teachers are quick to notice learning disabilities, but Brick is older than I am.

The computer screen changes color as I log in, and immediately I'm snapped back to reality when I see the numbers staring back at me. I gasp, wondering if this can be right. I don't know what I was expecting when Brick said he had some money. I do know that I sure as hell wasn't expecting this!

"Holy shit," comes Marvin's voice from behind me. "That's . . . that's almost a million dollars, Cop!"

"It's yours," says Brick without hesitation. "It'll take twenty-four hours for the bank to have the cash ready for me. I'll stay with you until then. You let everyone else go now. There'll never be a police report. I don't give a shit about the money. We don't give a shit about you."

I glance back at Marvin, and I can see that he's thinking hard. He turns to Glasses and the terrified family and shakes his head. "You've all seen our faces," he says slowly. "You'll be describing us to sketch artists and scanning through mugshots the moment we let you go."

"They won't be calling the police," I blurt out, not sure how I'm sounding so confident. I look over at Glasses and his family. "They just want this to be over. You haven't hurt them. You haven't stolen from them. You know where they live, and they're scared of you. What's the other option? You're going to just shoot us all? Have the best forensics experts in the state all over this place? Have the FBI start a massive manhunt? You think that's a better plan than to simply trust us and walk away with a million dollars, no strings attached, no police involved?"

"You got a cop right there," Mug growls from the background, pointing at Brick. He scratches his head with his gun in a way that makes me wonder if he's all there. "You don't think he's gonna file a report? Hah!"

Brick stands and turns to face them. He steps in front of me, and I feel his broad body cast a shadow over me like a shield. I feel protected. I feel safe. I feel like I'm . . . I'm . . . his.

Ohgod, I'm *his*!

A ripple of excitement goes through me as I stand behind Brick, marveling at how his broad frame perfectly covers my body. I can't help but think back to that kiss, that moment when the world melted away like it was all make-believe, like all of this is just the twisted path that fate takes to bring two lovers together.

"I can't file a report," comes Brick's voice, breaking me from my daydream. "Not after I give you the money."

"Why not?" says Marvin.

Brick snorts. "How do you think I got all that money?"

It takes them a moment, and then Marvin grins and shakes his head. "A dirty cop!" he says.

"Right," says Brick, and although I can tell he's lying, Marvin and Mug clearly believe him. "So you get it now? I can't report you guys without exposing myself too. Even if I don't tell anyone about the money, if you guys get caught, then *you'll* tell them! So I'd be fucked anyway." Then he turns to Glasses and the family, narrowing his eyes in a way that almost makes me laugh because it's so fake. "For the same reason I can't let these guys file a report. And if they do, I'll dispute their testimony. Discredit them. Make their lives a living hell."

Marvin is slowly nodding his head. I look up at Brick, my own eyes narrowing, but in admiration. Brick isn't dumb at all, I realize. Yes, I know he's lying about being a bad cop—I just know it. But he's serious about not reporting them. He's serious about not giving a shit about the money. He's a protector, and his instincts to protect me, to protect these kids . . . it's real and strong. It's beautiful.

The room is silent for a long, tense moment. Then Marvin nods and exhales. "We gotta roll the dice," he says. "The bitch and the dirty cop are both right. We kill anyone, and the FBI will hunt us down like dogs. And the cop can't report us without screwing himself over. All right, Mug. We're doing this." He thinks for a moment and then nods again. "It's gonna take twenty-four hours to get the cash? All right then. Make the withdrawal, Cop. I'm watching."

But Brick doesn't move, and I wonder if he's second guessing himself about handing over his life savings—or wherever that money came from—to some lowlifes.

"You call her a bitch again and I'll kill you," Brick says, his voice strained, his anger rising so fast I'm worried that he's going to leap across the room and get himself killed. I reach out my hand and place it against his hard back, and from the way he stiffens, I know my touch is the only thing that stopped him from losing control. Again I feel that warmth flow through me, and I swallow hard when I realize that Brick is willing to die to protect me, but at the same time is responsive to my touch.

I'm about to say that it doesn't matter what these assholes call me. Sticks and stones. I've been called worse by the kids on the playground back in grade school.

Big Beatrice.
Bea the Bear.
Burly Bea.
Who cares?

He cares, I think as I feel my touch calm Brick down. Slowly he turns back to the computer, his forehead crinkling with concentration as he pecks at the keys to make the withdrawal. Marvin is watching closely, but I can tell the criminal was taken aback by what he saw in Brick in that moment, what he heard in Brick's tone. He knows, just like I do, that Brick wasn't kidding. Brick is as capable of taking a life as either of these men.

The realization should terrify me, but it doesn't. It makes me feel safe, like there's nothing these men can do to me with Brick around.

"There," says Brick, leaning back and exhaling like

the focus on the numbers and letters was a tremendous effort for him. A moment later a notification pops up on the screen, and Brick's face goes red as he narrows his eyes and hesitates.

"It says the money will be available at your branch by this time tomorrow," I say, coming close to Brick and reading for him. I shiver with warm excitement as I feel his body relax. I know he's relieved that I stepped up and saved him from embarrassment. It's so silly, but I know it's meaningful. Somehow it makes me believe that maybe we *are* made for each other. He's never been able read properly, and if there's one thing I can do better than pretty much anyone in the world, it's read. I'm a librarian, for heaven's sake.

"Twenty four hours," Marvin grunts, stepping away and looking at his watch. He glances around the room, his jaw tight. Then he nods, turning to Mug and gesturing at the family, all of whom are still on the couch. "Down to the basement." He turns back to us. "You two are next."

I blink and swallow as Mug ushers the family down the stairs to the basement. Ten minutes later he's back, and then the two of them signal with their guns that it's time for us to head underground. I take a hesitant step forward, peering down into the basement and feeling a chill go through me. The basement is unfinished, and it looks dark. No windows. And did I say it looked dark?

"We can stay up here," I say to Marvin. I look toward the window. "The yard is big and there's a tall hedge near the fence. No one can see us from the street."

Marvin shakes his head. "No way. There might be folks knocking at the door today and tomorrow: delivery guys, neighbors, friends. Anyone stopping by needs to think there's nobody home. Basement. Now. Don't make me ask again."

I feel Brick step close to me, and a moment later his big arm slides around my waist. I frown and look up at him, and I see his eyes soften. Ohmygod, does he know? Does he know my most embarrassing secret? That even though I'm a strong, independent woman (well, kinda independent—I'm about to be fired and evicted. Oops!), I get claustrophobic in small, dark spaces? I always have. Yeah. I'm basically scared of the dark. There, I said it. To myself, at least.

"You'll be with me, Bea," he says softly, with a confidence that almost makes me forget that we're being held at gunpoint, and we probably don't get to make the rules. He looks at Marvin, his gaze firm, his voice tight with authority. "She'll be with me."

Marvin blinks, and I sense him back down instinctively to Brick's authority. He thinks for a moment, and then nods. "Laundry room," he says hoarsely to Mug before turning back to us. "Laundry room," he says again. Then, after clearing his throat and deepening his voice like this is his idea, he says, "Both of you. Together."

8

<u>BRICK</u>

At least we're together, I think as I look around the laundry room in the unfinished basement. It's basically a storage closet, with no windows. The walls are exposed stone, part of the original foundation. I'm not punching my way out of here.

Satisfied that we're safe for now at least, I turn my attention to Bea. She's standing in the middle of the cramped space, staring up at a solitary lightbulb that's swinging from a wire.

"It's dead," she says, a shiver in her voice like she's trying to control herself. She reaches up and pulls at the string that operates the switch. Just a click and nothing else. "They must have left it on when they went on vacation. Idiots. How do you not turn off the lights before you leave the house?!"

I take a breath as I watch her reach up above her head again. That gray skirt is riding up her solid thighs, and I almost groan out loud when I see her perfectly formed ass and legs flex and tighten as she goes up on her toes and tries to reach for the bulb. Finally I step up and reach above her head for her, twisting the bulb in case it was just loose. Nope. It's dead.

"There's enough light," I say softly, glancing at the frosted glass window above the locked door. Light from the rest of the basement is casting a dim glow over the laundry room. There's also some sunlight somehow making its way in from the stairway and passage. "We'll be fine, Bea. Those guys aren't going to mess with us. It'll be over in a few hours."

"In a few hours the sun will be gone and it'll be dark," Bea says. "And what if the lights in the basement go out?"

I frown again as I look at the fear on her pretty face. "Wait," I say slowly, rubbing my chin. "Are you . . . are you afraid of the dark?"

She turns to me, her red lips pursed tight, her fists clenched like she's about to lose her shit. "Yes!" she says, her voice peaked. "Yes, OK? Laugh all you want, but I can't help it! I had a bad experience as a kid, and I . . . you know what, never mind. We need to get out of here, Brick! I can't be in here! Break this door down! Do something!"

"No," I say, shaking my head and taking another step toward her. "I can't risk a fight. There's too many people in this house. No way I'm fighting my way out without someone getting hurt. And I can't risk that. I won't risk that. I may be dumb, but I'm not *that* dumb."

Bea blinks at my last sentence, calming down almost instantly as her focus turns to me. Her face softens as she looks up at me. "You've said that a couple of times—that you're dumb. But you're not. I saw how you dealt with those men up there, Brick. I saw how you controlled your emotions, didn't just lose your shit and try to fight your way out, getting us all killed in the bargain. I saw how you stepped in and solved the problem in a way that gives us all a shot at just walking away without a scratch." She shakes her head again, reaching up and touching my cheek in a way that makes me shudder. "You aren't dumb, Brick. You're just dyslexic."

I blink and cock my head. "I'm what?"

"Dyslexic," she says, her eyes wide as she shrugs. "Didn't you know? Weren't you diagnosed in school?"

I snort. "School? Bea, I was home schooled by my mom." I shake my head as I try not to think back to those years. "If you can call being yelled at by a drunk woman all day and then whipped by a raging alcoholic of a dad most of the night being schooled." I grunt as I feel myself bury the memory again. I got good at that. We do what we need to do to survive. We become what we need to become.

Bea inhales sharply, her palm stroking my face as I tense up at the memory and then slowly relax because of what I see in this woman's eyes. Compassion. Understanding. And . . . and . . . and love?

"My parents were drunks too," she says softly, a shadow passing behind her big round eyes. "I used to beg them not to drink, and they'd lock me in the bathroom so I'd shut up about it." She swallows hard, shooting a quick glance up at the dead lightbulb. "One night they locked me in there and passed out. There was a storm outside, and the power went out. The lights went out. I banged on the door to be let out, but nobody came. I thought my parents had left me. I thought maybe they'd died." She closes her eyes and lowers her voice. "I *wished* they were dead."

"Me too," I whisper, reaching for Bea's face and cupping her soft cheeks in my big hands. We just look into one another's eyes, and I blink as I see tears roll down her cheeks. What's happening here? I've known this woman for a day, and already I feel like I've known her forever. Like I want her forever. Like she's mine forever.

She snorts and forces a smile, clearing her throat and burrowing her head into my broad chest. "Are we seriously bonding over wishing our parents were dead?" she says, trying to laugh away the depth of the moment.

I stroke her hair, leaning down and kissing her gently on the head. I take a deep breath, her scent filling my lungs, overwhelming my senses, making me forget about our situation, about the danger that awaits us tomorrow. Bea is right. I'm not an idiot. I know what Marvin is probably thinking about right now. I saw the way his eyes glazed over when he saw my bank balance. He wasn't expecting to score that kind of money. No fucking way. That kind of money is probably beyond his wildest dreams. It's the kind of money that changes people. Turns good men into monsters. So what will it do to a bad man like Marvin? What's it doing to him as he thinks about it all night, as the thought of him sharing it with Mug eats away at his insides?

I push away the thought that in twenty-four hours I might be fighting for my life, fighting for *her* life. Then I smile as I feel Bea burrow into my large body like a little girl. But she's not a little girl. She's a woman with real strength, real character, real courage.

And real curves, I think as my hands slowly move down her back, tracing their way along her sides, stopping at her hips as I feel a rush of arousal that blasts me to a different level. Suddenly I want to take her, make her mine, my balls tensing up with an urgency that makes me wonder what just happened. I blink as those images of Bea pregnant with my babies flickers through like sunlight coming through the trees, and then I understand what's happening. It's instinct. Instinct that's primal, ancient, ingrained deep in the psyche of the animals we are, the animal I am, the man I am.

Then I understand that no matter what happens tomorrow, Bea is going to get out of here alive. I don't give a shit if everyone else is dead at the end of it, so long as Bea is alive.

Because she's going to be carrying something for me at the end of the night.

Carrying something for us.

"Brick," she whispers as my hands cup her ass from behind and squeeze hard. "Brick, what are you doing?"

"You know what I'm doing," I growl, sliding my hands under her skirt and grinding my cock between her hips. "Do you want me to stop?"

She looks up at me, her eyes unfocused from the arousal that I can feel coursing through her curves, the need that I can sense in her being, the instinct of the woman in her rising up so strong I can fuck-ing *smell* it. She doesn't answer my question, and I clench my jaw and look down at her, giving her one more chance to tell me to stop, to stop before I can't stop, before I *won't* stop. Not until she's mine, inside and outside. Now and forever. Mine in a way that nobody can challenge, nobody can take away, not now, not ever.

She groans as I dig my fingers into her soft, beautiful ass from behind, yanking her panties up so they ride deep into her rear crack. I can already feel her wetness on her soft inner thighs between her legs. I can already smell her feminine musk calling to me like a drug. I want to drink from her. Eat her up. Swallow her whole. Fucking *possess* her.

She looks up at me, her eyelids fluttering, her lips trembling like she's trying to say something. But I shake my head and grin down at her.

"Time's up," I whisper, leaning close to her lips, so close I can feel her breath on my face. "I'm not stopping, Bea. I'm going to make you mine. Right now. Right here. This might be all we have, Bea. This one night might be our always, might be our forever, might be everything, Bea."

Her eyelids flicker open, and she nods like she knows what I say is true, like she feels the urgency just like I do.

"Then make it count," she whispers, the words coming from so deep inside her I know we're past the point of thinking. Now it's just feeling. Just instinct. Just need. "Make it count."

I grin as if my woman has just issued me a challenge, and I feel the world contract around us, like nothing else is real except this one moment, this one moment that needs to capture forever. Make it count, I think as I grip her panties firmly from behind and slowly rip them down the seams as my cock throbs against her mound. Make it count.

And then I kiss her. I kiss her like it's the last time I'll ever kiss her. I kiss her. By God, I kiss her.

9
BEA

I kiss him back with an urgency that seems to come from outside me, or perhaps from so deep inside that I can't even understand it. I feel the urgency in Brick's kiss too, in his touch, the way he's clawing at my ass like a beast, rubbing his hard cock against my mound and making me so wet I want to wail out loud.

"Shhh," I moan as Brick pulls my ripped panties off me and growls as he unbuckles his heavy equipment belt and lets it drop to the hard floor. "They'll hear us!"

"Let them hear us," he mutters, unzipping his pants as he leans in and kisses me hard on the mouth again. "This isn't your library, Miss Bea. We're gonna scream, shout, fucking *roar*."

"Um, I don't *roar*," I say with a giggle—a giggle that quickly turns to a gasp as Brick steps back and pulls his shirt off, rips off his bulletproof vest, tears off his undershirt until he's standing before me naked as the day, a wall of hard muscle, cock standing straight out, the biggest cock I've ever seen, bouncing gently, its shaft thick like a pillar, its tip dark red and glistening with his need. "Oh, my God," I whisper. Now I *want* to roar! Roar like a lioness in heat, a she-beast about to be taken by her mate. "Oh, God, Brick!"

He stands there before me in all his glory, and I know he's mine. I can't explain it, but there's no doubt that this is my man, that I'm his woman, that no matter what happens, we're together right now and we'll be together forever. All those old books that talk about fate, destiny, meant-to-be? They were right. I see it right here before me.

I feel my wetness drip down my naked thighs as Brick takes a step towards me. In the dim light he looks like some kind of dark god, I think, and my mouth just hangs open as I take in the sight of his massive pectorals, tight nipples perched on top of a chest that looks like slabs of granite, a stomach flat like a workman's bench, rippled and contoured like a Renaissance artist's study of the human body. His scent comes to me as he leans close and grasps me by the back of the neck, and I inhale deep so his aroma fills my lungs.

He kisses me again, and I moan as I taste his clean mouth, feel his tongue push its way past my lips like he's tasting me, savoring me, consuming me. He pulls at my hair from behind, and then he's squeezing my boobs, pinching my nipples through my top until they harden to points, like they're standing at attention, responding to his touch in the most exhilarating way.

"This comes off," he whispers, grabbing my arms and raising them above my head. "I need to see you, Bea. All of you."

I blink and look away. I'm so hot for him that a part of me wants to be free of these clothes so I can spread wide for my man. But I swallow hard as I wonder if he's going to like what he sees. I've accepted my body for what it is, but it's another matter to know if—

"Fuck, you're beautiful," comes his voice, and when my eyelids flicker and my vision comes back into focus, I realize Brick has already slipped my top up over my head and tossed it onto the dryer in the corner. He's staring down at my heavy boobs, cupping them in his big hands and massaging them hard, his thumbs grinding down on my nipples. "Beautiful and mine, Bea. Mine, you hear?"

"OK," I say, barely able to say more than that, my eyes rolling up in my head as another moan escapes from my lips. A moment later I'm gasping in shock as Brick rips my bra open down the middle so my boobs pop out like they're being released from prison. "That bra doesn't open from the front," I mutter as I watch Brick lean in and take my left nipple into his mouth, his hands reaching down and moving up my skirt until he's got one hand on my ass, the other fingering me between my legs.

Brick just grunts as he sucks my nipples so hard I think he's going to swallow me whole. I look down and blink in shock at the way my body is responding to him. My nipples look dark red in the dim light, big like saucers, nubs pert and stiff. My skin is glistening with his saliva, and although it should feel sick, I love it. I feel like he's marking me, claiming me, owning me. I think back to how he just called me beautiful, and I suddenly *feel* beautiful, like I suddenly understand what it means to feel beautiful.

I'm smiling wide as Brick pushes me against the wall and goes down on his knees, his tongue tracing its way down along my bare belly, circling my belly button, teasing the waistband of my skirt, which is raised up over my hips.

"You smell so good," Brick whispers as he kisses my

mound gently, his tongue expertly sliding through my matted curls and finding my clit. "And you taste like—"

But he doesn't finish the sentence because he's jammed his face between my legs, slamming me against the wall and driving his tongue deep into my cunt with a suddenness that makes me choke. I open my mouth to scream as I feel my orgasm rolling in like distant thunder, and although there's a little voice inside that tells me I need to stay quiet, I know I'm not going to be able to hold back. Not with Brick doing what he's doing. Wait, what *is* Brick doing?

I frown as I realize he's pulled his tongue out of me, and a wave of anger rushes through me as I feel my pussy yearn to be filled again. Brick's still on his knees, but he's leaning off to the side, reaching for something. Reaching for my torn panties.

"Open up," he says with a grin, his long arm reaching up with those panties.

"What?" I mutter, my mind still swirling as I feel my climax hovering in the distance like it's just waiting to come crashing in, destroying everything in its path like a tidal wave. "What are you—"

And then Brick stuffs my panties into my mouth, and before I can protest he's back down between my legs, fucking me with his tongue, furious and fierce, his hands pulling my asscheeks apart from behind, his fingers circling my rear hole.

"Now you can scream, my little librarian," he growls into my pussy just before sliding his stiff, thick tongue back inside and curling it against the front wall of my vagina, finding my g-spot and tapping it as my

wetness pours all over his face like a river breaking
through a dam. "Now you can scream."

As he speaks I feel my climax roar in, and I lean my
head back and scream. The sound comes out muffled,
and I almost gag on my own panties as I come all over
Brick's face. I feel my knees buckle as my orgasm hits
me like a truck, but Brick's holding me firmly by my
hips as he drinks from me like some kind of wild animal. I'm taking heaving, desperate breaths, inhaling
the scent of my own wetness from my soaked panties. It feels filthy and I come again, my body thrash-
ing as Brick takes me to a place of ecstasy I didn't
know existed.

"Brick, I . . . I can't even . . ." I gurgle through my
gag as my climax crests and breaks, shattering me as
I put my hands on his massive shoulders to steady
myself. "Oh, God, Brick, that feels like—"

But I don't finish the sentence, because Brick is on
his feet again, kissing me hard on the lips as he reaches between us and lines his cock up with my slit. I feel
his need, and I just blankly nod as he pushes himself
into me in a smooth upward motion that stretches
me so damned wide I just gurgle like I'm drowning.

Brick pulls the panties out of my mouth, and I take
deep, heaving breaths as he kisses my face, bites my
neck, holds me against the wall and pushes so deep
into me that I swear I feel him in my throat.

He holds himself inside me, his cock somehow feeling like it's getting bigger, its girth pushing against
my inner walls, stretching the mouth of my vagina
in a way I didn't think was possible. He's big, I real-

ize through my delirium. And he's not sure if I can take him. If I can handle everything he's got to give.

"Are you OK, Bea?" he whispers, his hard body shuddering as if he's using all his willpower to hold back, to give me time to understand what's coming, to give my body time. "Can I . . . I want to . . . oh, hell, Bea, I need to . . ."

"Yes," I whisper, my mouth hanging open. I can barely even see. "Whatever you need, Brick. I'm yours, Brick. I'm yours."

10

<u>BRICK</u>

I'm yours," she whispers to me, and it's the last thing I hear before everything goes silent, like someone's just turned off the sound. But I don't need sound. I don't need sight. Not when it feels like this.

My cock flexes inside her as I kiss her face and neck, and slowly I begin to pump my hips. She stiffens as I push deep into her, but I feel her nod against my chest and I know she can take me. She was built for me. She's mine. Fucking *mine*!

I feel her pussy tighten around my shaft as if she can hear my thoughts, as if she's feeling the same urgency I am, a need to mate that's so primal that it seems to come from a place that's old, ancient, eternal. I look into her eyes as I pull back and thrust once more, and I nod as if I know what I'm feeling is true. It's real. More real than life. More real than death.

It's love, I think as I pull her hair back from her forehead and look upon her pretty face. I can feel my hips thrusting harder, pumping faster, my balls slapping up against her as I prepare to fill her with my seed. But it also seems like time has slowed down, like we're living a lifetime in this moment, experiencing eternity in each other's eyes, loving each other with an intensity that not everyone is blessed with.

"I love you," I whisper, looking into her eyes as I feel her wetness flow down my shaft, feel the shudder of her thighs as I push against her, feel how her bosom is warm against my hard chest, her breath hot against my glistening neck. She was made for me, body and soul, and although I know it's crazy, I say it again. "I love you, Bea. I . . . shit, I—"

"I love you too, Brick," she whispers back, looking up into my eyes as I hold her hair back from her face. "I don't know how I know, but I know. I love you. Oh, God, I . . ."

Her eyes roll up in her head as she comes in my arms, her orgasm rising up and taking her in a way that makes me want to roar in pleasure. It's been a while since I took a woman, but with everyone before her it was always about me, my pleasure, me taking what I want. This . . . this is different. With Bea I want to *give* pleasure, make her whimper, make her wail, make her come again and again until she can't take any more. And then I'll give her more.

I'm still pushing into her as she thrashes against the wall, but now I've slowed down into a powerful, deep-driving rhythm, my fingers caressing her sides, digging into her hips, clutching at her love-handles as I feel my cock seek out every inch of her secret space, like I'm claiming her from the inside. I lick her neck, kiss her cheeks, push my tongue into her mouth and taste her with a hunger that makes me growl. My balls are tightening, but I flex my cock as if I want to hold back, prolong this moment, make this last forever. I already feel my semen rising up along my shaft, like my body is yearning to pour its seed into my mate, fill her until she overflows, do what it was born to do.

"Oh, shit, Brick, I'm still coming," she whimpers as she breaks from the kiss and leans her head back, her eyes closed tight, her mouth twisted in a grimace of pure ecstasy. "How can I still be . . . oh, *God*!"

The sound of the pleasure in her voice drives me close to madness, and I pull out of her and drop to my knees again, jamming my face between her legs and opening my mouth wide, breathing deep from her sex, swallowing like I want to drink from her, want her inside me just like I want to be inside her. She's grinding her hips into my face, coming all over my lips, coating my stubble with her juices, almost suffocating me as she clamps her strong thighs tight around my head.

I hold my face there for a long moment, feeling Bea's climax finally shatter and begin to wind down. My own need is rising like the swell of the ocean, and I'm so far gone I couldn't remember where I was if I tried. With a gasp I pull my face out from between her legs, feeling her tangy sweetness on my tongue, licking my lips to get more of her taste inside me. Through my blurred vision I see her beautiful slit laid bare before me, bright and clean, smiling like a red crescent moon though her wet pubic curls. I rub her thighs again and turn her around, groaning as I firmly grasp her big round ass, squeeze her smooth buttocks, marveling at how perfectly her rear globes fit in my big paws. Before I know it my face is in there, right between her buttcheeks as I spread her from behind. Then I'm licking her rear pucker like a goddamn animal, and I feel her tense up in shock.

"What are you doing?" she whispers, her voice trembling as I circle her clean dark rim with my tongue. "Oh, God, Brick. That feels . . . it feels so . . . so . . ."

"I want to own every part of you," I mutter, pulling my face away and staring at her beautiful rear pucker glistening with my saliva. Then I reach one hand beneath her and finger her pussy, slowly massaging her asshole with my other thumb, teasing her as I feel my cock throb so hard it's bouncing up and down on its own. I rub her mound roughly from beneath, slowly pushing the thumb of my other hand into her rear until she relaxes, pushes her ass up, and with a shuddering moan comes again.

"There we go," I whisper as she convulses against the wall, her fingers clawing at the exposed stone, her head half-turned, eyes wide and delirious like she's shocked I made her come like that, from doing what I'm doing.

And I want to do it. I want to own her in every fucking way. But I'm not going to take her there. My body won't allow it. Not today. I need to put my seed where it belongs.

Just a little while more, I think as my balls tighten again. I know that the moment I push myself back into her I'm going to come like a goddamn stallion, come so hard I might damn well pass out. Slowly I rise to my feet, sliding my arms around Bea's waist and turning her, fingering her slit again as I grasp my heavy cock with my other hand.

Then I feel Bea's fingers intertwined with mine, and I groan as I see that she's looking down between my legs, her eyes glazed over with pleasure. She wants to touch me, I realize. All right.

I nod as I take my hand away, gritting my teeth as Bea's soft hands stroke me until I almost blast my load right at her. But I clench my balls and hold on, nodding as Bea slowly goes down to her knees.

"I want to . . ." she whispers as she brings her red lips close to my oozing cockhead. "Brick, I want to . . ."

"Go on," I growl down at her, nodding as I slowly slide my fingers through her hair until I'm holding her head firmly. She looks exquisite from this angle, her boobs hanging off to either side, her thighs spread wide. I know she wants me to come inside her, but she also wants to taste me. Just like I needed to taste her, she needs to taste me. It's filthy, but the need is so raw that it feels pure, natural, goddamn perfect.

"Oh, fuck, that's perfect, Bea," I groan as she slowly takes me into her mouth, her lips dragging along my throbbing shaft, her tongue rolling against my sensitive tip. "You're perfect. Just perfect."

My grip on her head tightens as she begins to suck me, and soon I'm pumping into her, feeling her throat open as she takes me in a way that makes me feel . . . loved. Loved?

Yes, loved.

Loved like I've never been loved.

Loved like it's the first time.

Loved like it's forever.

11

BEA

It feels like love, I think as I close my eyes and take Brick into my mouth. My body is still humming from the way he just made me come . . . come in the most filthy way possible. I've never let a man touch me there. Even the thought of it was a non-starter for me. But Brick did it with what I know is love, like he wanted to taste every part of me, like he wants to know all my secrets, possess my body and my soul and everything in between.

And I want to feel every part of him in every part of me, I think as I open my throat and suck him hard, taking his massive cock so far into my mouth I can feel his heavy balls press against my chin. His musk smells clean and thick, like a man. Like *my* man.

My pussy clenches I feel Brick grip my head and begin to thrust, and I know he's going to come soon. A part of me wants to feel him explode against the back of my throat, wants to swallow his heat as he roars at the way I'm pleasuring him. But there's a deeper part of me that yearns to take his seed, is desperate to take his seed, *needs* to have him put his seed where it belongs. It sounds like madness, and perhaps it is. But hell, *all* of this is madness, isn't it? In fact it's so crazy it's almost planned! Is that how fate works?

I smile as I feel that confidence return, a sense that this is all about us, just the universe playing a love song with our lives. But then I hear a sound outside the door, and suddenly fear whips through me as I remember in a flash where we are, what's happening in our lives, that we're in danger, that we might be dead in a few hours!

Brick hears it too, and suddenly he pulls out of my mouth, a long trail of saliva and pre-cum still connecting his cock to my lower lip as I sit there on my knees. Incredibly the fear hasn't killed my arousal, and when I feel my pussy clench again, I realize that the urgency has actually *increased* my need!

One look at Brick and I know he's feeling the same way. The real world can wait. This is about us, about our union. Whatever's happening outside that door isn't going to stop us, can't stop us, *won't* stop us.

The doorknob is moving like someone's about to push it open, and I blink as I desperately look for my clothes in the dark. I'm about to just crawl into a corner, hunch into a ball, and cover myself as best I can; but then Brick just shakes his head and points.

I stare as Brick, naked and magnificent, cock hard and bouncing, strides over to a wooden chair against the far wall. He grabs the chair, and a moment later he's jammed the back of the chair against the doorknob so whoever it is can't come inside. Then he turns and looks at me, his eyes narrowed, his jaw tight, every muscle in his body flexed, his cock standing straight up. I know what he's asking. I know what he's saying. I know what he wants.

And I want it too.

Slowly I get to my feet, standing as straight as I can, upright and naked. I brush a strand of hair from my face and clear my throat. There's a hint of self-consciousness as I see Brick's gaze drop to that dark space between my legs, but I manage to smile and let him look, let him look at his woman. I've never done that for a man, let him gaze at my naked body like that. But Brick isn't any man. He's my man. He's my forever.

"What?" I say, blinking as I meet his gaze.

He takes a step towards me, and I blink again as I hear the men outside the door.

"We can't!" I whisper, taking a step back even though I'm hot for him, wet for him, the danger making my arousal soar in a way I didn't think would happen. "They'll hear us, Brick!"

"No, they won't," says Brick, moving closer, faster, gripping me by the hips, his hands moving around to my ass. "Up you go."

I gasp as Brick grabs me from my ass and thighs and lifts me up, right off my feet, carrying me like I'm light as a feather! I almost squeal in surprise, but then gasp again when he puts me down on top of the dryer that's in the far corner of the laundry room.

The cool metal of the dryer makes me jump, but Brick reaches past me and flips the dial and turns it on, filling the room with noise as the vibrations make my body shiver in the most wonderful way.

Then Brick is up against me, pushing me backwards as the dryer heats up beneath my ass as if he's turned it to full-power, high-heat, super-cycle. A moment later he's sucking my boobs, pinching my nipples, spreading my thighs until I just give in and part my legs.

He pauses for a moment, his cock standing straight out over my mound, balls full and heavy between his legs. I can feel my slit open wide for him, wet and ready, ready to take him, take all of him.

"This is sick," I mutter as I know what's about to happen. "We can't, Brick. We . . . we . . . we . . . oh, Brick. Oh, *Brick*!"

He drives his ramrod-straight cock right into me without another word, and I arch my neck back at the sensation of my cunt being filled so fast, so deep, so hard. I've had sex before, but I swear this feels like I'm being taken for the first time, being opened up for the first time, being entered for the first time.

The dryer is hot below my naked ass, its roar filling the room with white noise that drowns out every other sound. Suddenly it feels like we're alone again, like it's just the two of us, like this is our goddamn story and everyone else is just gonna have to wait! I feel myself losing my grip on reality, and although I panic for a moment, the fear is gone as I feel Brick's warmth, feel his protection, feel his love.

And so I just close my eyes, wrap my legs tight around his muscular ass, and let him take me, let him have him, let him love me.

12

<u>BRICK</u>

I love her, I think, and it's so clear to me that I feel my face explode in a grin. Then I'm coming, suddenly, hard, so fucking hard the world just goes black around me. I choke at first, and then I lean my head back and shout as my balls seize up and deliver a load so big into Bea that I wonder if they emptied on the first shot. I hear her scream too, but the sound of the dryer drowns us out, and so I keep pumping into her as I roar, as she howls, as I blast load after load into her warm depths, feeling her tight pussy milking my cock like it's coaxing every last drop out of me.

"Oh, God, Bea," I gasp, blinking wildly as I feel her fingernails tear into my back, her heels dig into my ass, her thighs clamp tight on my hips as I ram into her so hard the dryer is rocking back and forth. "Oh, *fuck*!"

She's coming again too, I know, and I groan as I feel her wetness flow down my shaft, coating my balls as they seize up again and pour more of my semen into her. Soon she's overflowing down my cock, but I can't stop. I just shake my head and keep thrusting as she screams and thrashes, pouring more of my seed into her as if this is for keeps, the first time and the last time, always and forever in one moment.

This moment.

Our moment.

13
BEA

This is our moment, I think as I feel Brick explode inside me with such force that I almost black out. I can't see, I can barely breathe, and it feels like the whole world just exploded alongside. But at the bottom of it all there's a calmness, a rock-solid foundation to the chaos of what's happening, and as I let my orgasm wash over me even as my man pumps and thrusts, filling me with his seed in the most perfect way, I know that everything we've felt over the past day has been real.

"It's real, Brick," I whisper as he arches his body back and pushes the last of his load into me as my pussy tightens around his mast like it's squeezing everything out of him. "It's all real. It's all perfect."

Brick looks at me with glazed eyes, his smile slowly breaking as beads of sweat roll down his forehead from how hard he's been fucking me. The dryer is still bumping and whirring beneath me, warming me even as it rocks me back and forth. Brick is still inside me, and he holds himself there for a long time as we look into each other's eyes.

Then suddenly the dryer stops and there's dead silence in the little laundry room. I hold my breath and look past Brick's shoulder towards the door. Nothing. No movement. No sound.

"Maybe they've gone," I say with a giggle, not sure why this feels so weirdly funny. Perhaps I *have* gone insane. Maybe the stress caused a psychotic break, and I'm gonna spend the rest of my life in a lunatic asylum, wearing floral gowns and wistfully telling my fellow mental patients about the love of my life from years ago as the doctors smile and shake their heads in pity.

"Yeah, right," says Brick, slowly pulling out of me like he doesn't want to return to reality either. "Come on. Let's find your clothes. If those assholes break in here and see you like this, I swear I'll kill them with my bare hands."

I giggle again, this time at how Brick's face clouds over with anger at the thought of someone else seeing me naked. His possessiveness makes me feel loved, even though I know it's lame and silly. But I can't help it.

"No, you won't. You're not some dumb animal," I tease, still sitting on the dryer as Brick parades around naked, squinting in the dark as he looks for my clothes.

I see him flinch at the word "dumb," and I tense up. "That's not what I meant," I say quickly. "That you're dumb. I mean you're *not* dumb! I mean—"

I feel my panties come flying across the room, landing smack against my mouth as I squeal in surprise. I pull them away and hold them up, raising an eyebrow at Brick as he stands there naked, hands on his hips, long cock hanging down, a cocky grin on his face from how my panties are ripped down the middle.

"I take it back," I say with a sigh. "You *are* an animal. Now I'm going to be a hostage without panties?"

"You're not going to be a hostage at all," he says, his grin fading as he reaches for his own clothes. "You aren't leaving my side, Bea. I don't give a fuck what those guys threaten to do to me."

"Speaking of those guys," I say as I slip off the dryer

and pick up my skirt. "Where are they? I don't hear anything outside the door."

Brick slowly goes to the door and listens before shaking his head. "Dead calm outside." Then he glances up at the wooden ceiling and frowns. I listen, and sure enough, I hear the creaking of footsteps.

"They're upstairs," I say, exhaling as I put my skirt and blouse back on. It's only after I take a couple of breaths that I realize how tense I was. "What's the time?"

Brick glances at his watch and grunts. "We got plenty of time." He's got his pants on now, and is putting his equipment belt back on. They've taken his gun and radio, of course, but he smiles as he pulls something out and holds it up. "Hey! We got light!" he says, flicking on the flashlight and shining it right into my eyes.

"OK, don't do that!" I say, shielding my face and turning from the bright light. I open my eyes when he shines it away from me, and as the beam illuminates the little room, I see something in the corner. "Hey, what's that?"

Brick shines the light over in that direction and grunts again. "It's a book. I hate books."

I turn and look over at him. My immediate reaction is to get annoyed, but then I just laugh. Of course he hates books. Books are what made him think he was dumb. And of *course* fate has put the two of us together: A librarian and a dyslexic.

"Well, I love books, and you're going to love them too," I say, walking over and bending down to pick up the book, probably left there by one of the kids. I feel Brick point the flashlight right at my ass as my skirt rides up, and I quickly stand back up and turn to him with a fake frown on my face. "OK, that's just juvenile," I say as Brick gives me a wolfish grin and then focuses the flashlight on my boobs, which are loose and heavy since this beast ripped my bra in two as well. "You know, if you're going to act like a child, then I'm going to treat you like a child. Come here. Sit."

He frowns as I point at a spot on the floor. Then he sighs and sits, crossing his legs and leaning against the wall. I sit down in front of him, my back toward him. Then I slowly lean back into his body, feeling the warmth of his presence envelop me as he pulls me close. He kisses my hair, and I reach up and guide his hand to where I want it.

"Right there," I say, making him position the flashlight just right as I hold the book up. I feel him tense up, but he does what I ask.

I glance at the cover of the book. It isn't a kid's book after all, and I blink as I read the title. It's called *The Bridge Across Forever*, and I get that strange feeling of familiarity, déjà vu of something you've never experienced before.

And then, even though I know we're hostages, our lives in danger, our deaths perhaps just hours away, I lower my voice and start to read. I read to him. To my man. To my love. To my forever.

I feel Brick's hard body relax as he cradles me, his breathing slowing down. I wonder if anyone's ever read to him before. Then I realize it doesn't matter. Our pasts don't matter, because nothing's going to change our future.

14
NINE HOURS LATER
BRICK

I open my eyes and look upon a sight that makes me want to cry. It's Bea, curled up on the floor, head on my lap, that book face-down on her round belly. In that moment I feel complete, and I try not to breathe so I can savor this moment no matter what happens in the next few hours.

"Thank you," I whisper to my sleeping beauty, gently brushing a strand of hair from her forehead. I really mean it. I feel so much gratitude that it's almost overwhelming. I'm thankful, pure and simple. Thankful that we had this moment together, had this night together, had this experience together.

I hear more sounds above me, and I frown as I count the footsteps. It sure as hell sounds like more than just Marvin and Mug up there. But they'd locked the family down at the far end of the basement, hadn't they? And Marvin was right about not having anyone up there where a visitor or mailman might notice. So what the fuck is happening?

I glance over at the door, my frown deepening as I realize the latch is in a different position. Then adrenaline rips through me when I realize the door is unlocked! Those dumb fucks must have forgotten to lock it again after trying to get in last night!

"Honey, wake up," I whisper urgently, tapping her on the arm.

"Did you just call me honey?" she says dreamily, and I glance down at her and smile when I realize she's been awake all this while, laying still against me, listening to me, taking it all in just like I've been doing.

A yearning ripples through me as I clench my jaw and think about how badly I want a future with Bea, how desperately I want to see the babies that I somehow know are already forming inside her womb, how deeply I want a life with her—a long life. Eternity is well and good, but I want my flesh-and-blood future too. I had already decided that no matter what, Bea wasn't going to get hurt. But now I decide I'm not going to die today either. Nope. I'm not leaving her, come what may. She's mine, and I'm not fucking leaving her.

I close my eyes and mutter a silent prayer. I'm not a religious man. I don't even know who the hell I'm praying to. But I pray anyway, pray that whoever or whatever brought us together does whatever's needed to *keep* us together. Then I slowly move from beneath my woman.

"Stay here," I say softly, reaching for my bulletproof vest that's lying a few feet away. "And put this on."

Bea snaps to attention, sitting up straight and turning to me. "What are you doing, Brick?"

"Just do what I say, Bea," I say, my voice issuing the command with such authority that she just blinks and stays quiet. I'm not going to argue. "Stay here, and don't come upstairs. No matter what you hear, all right?"

"That's ridiculous," she blurts out, pushing the vest away. "Wherever you're going, I'm coming with you."

I close my eyes and tighten my jaw. "Bea, this is not

the time to argue. I think I have a shot at ending this quickly. Just do what I say, and—"

"Ohmygod, the door's unlocked!" she says, finally noticing the turned latch. She looks back at me, panic racing through her when she realizes that I'm going to sneak upstairs and catch these assholes by surprise. "Brick, no! You'll be killed."

"I won't," I say firmly, not sure where that confidence is coming from. Sneaking up on two armed, ex-military men in a sunny living room? Probably not gonna work out in my favor. Probably stupid as fuck. But my name is Brick, ain't it? So what the hell.

"Fate has given me a shot," I whisper, looking at the unlocked door like it's beckoning to me. "I gotta take the shot, Bea. I gotta do it."

I look back at her, searching her face for some sign that she understands . . . understands that this is who I am: A protector, a fighter, a man of action. She's right that I'm not an idiot—after all, I played the mental game with these assholes when I knew I didn't have a chance to get them physically. But now I've got a shot. I can't pass up this shot. Who knows how the day will play out. I . . . I *have* to take the shot.

"This is who I am," I whisper to her, touching her face as I feel a desperate need for her to understand. I can't do this if she doesn't understand. "Every crisis situation presents a chance that seems crazy but has to be taken. You have to trust me, Bea. Trust me to protect you." I pause and swallow hard, glancing down at her belly and then back into her eyes. "Protect our future."

She cocks her head, her face going flush as if she

knows what I mean, no matter how fucking absurd it sounds. She closes her eyes and mutters something that sounds like "This is insane!" Then she opens her eyes and nods.

"All right," she says, and in that moment I know this is my woman, the only woman who can suck up her own fears and put our future in my hands, trust her man to protect her, protect her family, protect their forever. "All right, Brick," she says. "Go do what you need to do. But you wear the vest. You know that makes sense."

I cup her face in my hands and kiss her, savoring her sweet taste and swallowing like it's a magic potion. Then I nod and put on the vest, knowing that she's right. I'm probably going to take a couple of bullets before I overpower those goons, and I'm no good to her bleeding all over the place.

Slowly I go to the door and pull the chair away. I listen and nod. Then I turn to her one last time. She's smiling up at me, staring at me with pride, with admiration, with love.

"Make it count," she whispers. "Make it count, Brick."

15
BEA

I count the seconds until I hear the first sounds of a fight, and then the anxiety rips through me so hard I can't even think.

"What the fu—" comes Marvin's muffled voice, his sentence ending in a cracking noise that I swear is Brick's massive fist colliding with his poor jawbone. A heavy thud above my head tells me Marvin is down for the count, and I can't help but clench my fists in excitement.

Mug screams, and I close my eyes and pray I don't hear a gunshot. I tell myself that even if Mug gets a shot off, he'll probably miss. If he does hit Brick, chances are he'll only score a shot on the bulletproof vest. By then it'll be over. My man will win. I'm sure of it.

But the screams and shouts continue, and before I know it I've burst through the door and am racing up the stairs, almost choking with panic as I imagine Brick dead on the carpet. I'm ready to leap at Mug, rip him to pieces with my fucking fingernails if I have to. But then just before turning the corner to the living room I stop. I freeze. Not because I'm scared, but because I remember what Brick said to me just before going: About protecting me, protecting our family, protecting what he just put inside me even though there's no way we can know for sure.

"Oh, God," I whisper to myself as a sickening

thought comes over me. I look over to my left and see the side door leading outside, to freedom, to escape. Suddenly I think I know what Brick was doing. "He was creating a diversion!" I mutter in disbelief. "He wanted me to escape! But he couldn't tell me that, because I would never agree. So he made me believe he had a chance!" I'm almost beside myself with a mixture of rage and grief, and I'm finding it hard to breathe as I think that Brick would want me to save myself instead of acting like an idiot and rushing out there to fight a battle against armed military men!

I look towards the side door again, but I don't think I can do it. I won't do it. I'm not leaving my man. If he's dead, then so be it. I'll lay down beside him. Fuck it. Here goes.

I prepare myself to rush out from behind the wall, hopefully slam into Mug with such force that my weight knocks him off his feet. But then I hear voices . . . people talking, not screaming.

It's the family, I realize. The kids, the dad, even the silent mom! Then I remember hearing footsteps above us earlier in the morning—footsteps of more than two people. Finally I take a breath and almost faint when I smell fresh coffee in the air, breakfast sausage in a pan, eggs and waffles and . . . and . . . and what the *hell* is going on?!

" . . . we . . . we just couldn't go through with it, man," Mug is saying as I step out into plain view and almost fall down again when I see Brick standing there, tall like a building, broad like a bridge, in his blue uniform, fists clenched and bloodied.

Marvin is face-down on the carpet, his legs moving as he groans in pain. Mug is holding his nose in place, sputtering as he tries to speak through the blood. And the family is sitting around the breakfast table . . . the breakfast table which is set for eight people—all of us!

"It was weird," Mug is saying as I slowly walk over to Brick and stand by his side. I see his face light up when he sees me, but he stays quiet and I follow his lead. "Yeah, weird," Mug says again. "Maybe it was because we had so much time to think about what we were doing, you know? We never planned for hostages and all that shit. We never planned to hurt anyone. And then when we were up here alone, with two families locked up in the basement, it hit us that we're monsters!"

I frown, my eyes going wide as I listen to Mug. For some reason I notice how he said "two families" like it was obvious, and I blink and look up at Brick and then down at my belly.

"We lost our own families while we were overseas," Mug says, his gray eyes tearing up as he glances at the kids and then back at us. "Marvin's wife took his kids and left. I was already going through a divorce, and the judge gave my ex sole custody while I was gone. We lost our shit. Did things overseas that got us court-martialed and discharged with no benefits. We were angry at everyone. Everyone but ourselves." He smiles, his teeth stained with blood. "But last night, when it was just the two of us sitting in the dark, we got to talkin', you know. Got to thinking about how the fuck we got to this point." He pauses and shakes his head. "Then Marvin says maybe it's fate or some shit. Meant-to-be that this cop and his woman shows up, then the family walks in. It makes us see ourselves, you know? See that it's all our own choices. Our own fault. Shit, Marvin's wife woulda left him anyway—guy was a drunk. Never hit her or nothin', but never loved her either. And I was a shitty father, crappy husband. We wanted to blame the military, blame everyone else, blame the fucking world. But last night . . . I dunno, man. It was weird. Spiritual and shit. Like . . . like . . ."

Like fate, I think as I feel Brick's arm slide around my waist. I nod at Mug, somehow forgiving him right there even though it wasn't up to me to forgive him.

Mug finally gets a hold of himself and looks up at Brick. "I guess you gonna take us in now, huh?"

Brick takes a breath. He looks down at his bloodied fists, over at Marvin groaning on the floor. "Well, if I do, I gotta explain punching you guys out after you'd already stood down. That's police brutality, you know. And there's too much bad press about the police these days."

Mug blinks like he doesn't understand.

"I think he says you can go," I say softly. "Just behave from now on, OK?"

It sounds hokey and downright ridiculous, but I feel a swell of real emotion that's hard to ignore. I think back to that feeling that this was our story, mine and Brick's story, and I wonder if the choice we made to be together no matter what was going on around us changed the course of events, made this day play out the way it did, made this about love, forgiveness, and rebirth instead of violence, death, and hatred.

"C'mon Marvin," says Mug quickly, as if he's worried Brick's going to change his mind. "I'll bring the truck around."

"We'll take my car," says Brick, his voice steady and commanding. "But you two are in the backseat."

Mug looks up in panic. "But I thought you said you were gonna let us go!"

"I am letting you go," Brick says. "But I also gave you my word. So we're going to stop at the bank. I said the money's yours, and it's still yours. Think of it as me making sure you don't need to try stealing someone's goddamn TV again." He takes a breath, his expression turning serious, his voice dropping. "My father was military," he says. "I've seen what war can do to a man. What it can do to his wife. His kids. His family. It's not easy for anyone. Hopefully this will make it easier for you two. It *is* my father's money, after all. Maybe it's justice that it goes to two military brothers that got hit hard. Yeah, maybe this is justice, you know?" Then he stands up straight and salutes the bewildered Mug and the astonished Marvin. "Thank you for your service, Gentlemen. Now make sure you buckle up in the backseat. Safety first."

16

FOUR HOURS LATER

BRICK

"**O**K, that was ridiculous," Bea says as we watch Marv and Mug drive away in their red pickup truck—along with three grocery bags of my money. "It's one thing to let them go. But to give them the money too? That's just . . ."

"That's justice," I say as I pull away from the curb in my cruiser, my woman by my side.

"Um, how exactly is that justice for those guys? It's more justice than they deserve. Yes, they made the choice to back down from hurting anyone, but they still made the choice to break into that house to begin with."

"A choice that brought the two of us together," I say, reaching across for her hand.

Bea is quiet for a moment, and I know she's thinking the same thing I am: How weird has this day been?! It's just too weird to *not* have been planned by some mischievous powers!

"Actually, *we* made the choice that brought us together," Bea says.

"Which choice was that?"

"Well, your choice to offer me a ride, and my choice to accept it," Bea says triumphantly like she's won something.

I think back to that first meeting, which seems

years ago but also like it was yesterday. Oh fuck wait—
it *was* yesterday.

"Actually, I never offered you a ride," I say slowly,
furrowing my brow as I think carefully about what
we said to each other. "Nope. Didn't ask the question,
and you didn't answer. You just assumed I'd give you
a ride, and I assumed I was giving you a ride."

Bea snorts, but then she goes quiet again like she
knows I'm right. Our meeting wasn't even a choice,
in a way, was it? It was almost like we simply assumed
we belonged together. Always. Forever.

I glance at her as I hold her hand and drive through
town. I'm so sure we're going to be together that I
swear I want to stop the fucking car and ask her to
marry me right now. But I hold my horses and remind myself that it might be too much too soon for
this librarian. Just chill, Brick. Take it slow.

But I can't take it slow. I won't take it slow. This is
who I am. I don't think. I do. And I'm doing it. This is
my woman, and I'm locking her up, locking her down,
claiming her in the body, the spirit, and on paper.

"Um, why are we stopping here?" she says as I pull
around the corner and then stop right in front of City
Hall. "Brick, why are we stopping here!"

"I'm not going to even ask the question," I say, looking her right in the eyes with all the seriousness in me.

She gasps as I kick the door open and rush around
to the other side. A moment later she's in my arms,
and I'm running up the goddamn steps of City Hall
in my police uniform, my curvy librarian in my arms,
her face bright red with embarrassment, her hands
desperately pulling at the bottom of her skirt to keep
anyone from seeing up it.

"I'm not even going to ask the question," I say again after I head straight to the clerk and tell him to find us a witness and a judge and take care of business. "And you're not going to answer it."

17
<u>**BEA**</u>

But I answer the question anyway. I answer it the way I answered every question over this whirlwind past day, a day where we lived a lifetime's worth, discovered each other, discovered ourselves in each other.

"Yes," I say, swallowing hard as I hold my thighs firmly together, wondering what the stern-looking female judge might say if she knew I wasn't wearing panties. "Yes, I do."

Yes, I do.

Always yes.

Forever yes.

18

<u>BRICK</u>

Yes," she says, and my knees almost buckle as I hear myself say the same thing.

And then I'm carrying her back down the steps of City Hall. Carrying my *wife* down the stairs. Carrying my forever down the stairs.

I grin and kiss her as I remember how easy it is to get shit taken care of when you're wearing a uniform. Yeah, some cops abuse that privilege, and yeah, maybe this is pushing it a bit. But it's for love. All's fair for love. I'm sure that's in some book.

And someday, I think as I look into her eyes and see the love, maybe she'll read it to me.

∞

EPILOGUE
ONE YEAR LATER
BEA

I sigh as I finish breastfeeding my two little ones and put them back in their adjoining rockers. The library lets me use a private office as my nursery, and so I bring the twins to work every day. Brick just got promoted to Lieutenant, and he doesn't have much time to look after the kids during the day.

Not that Brick needs to work, of course. After we got married, he explained that his inheritance was a trust fund, which meant that it pays out interest to him every month. The money he'd given away was just all the payments that he hadn't spent! Brick is . . . he's *rich*! I guess it means *we're* rich, but I don't think about that. We spend modestly, and the rest is put away. You never know when you'll need it.

I hum a soft lullaby to my twins, smiling as I see their father's eyes on our daughter Brenna, see Brick's thick black hair on Brock, our son. My forever is here. My story is over. This is my happy ending. So why do I have this strange feeling of melancholy?

"Is it postpartum?" I wonder aloud as I slowly close the door and leave my kids alone, checking to make sure the baby monitor is on while I head back to the stacks upstairs to dust off some of our older volumes.

But as I enter the silent stacks of the upper library, the stillness in the air reminds me of that laundry room where Brick and I were trapped on our first day together. And then suddenly I'm taken back to the madness of that day, the urgency of our first coupling, the raw, primal needs of our bodies, the way we possessed each other with such desperation, gave ourselves to one another with such abandon.

"That's what's missing—the excitement of that first meeting, the danger, the sense that we had to claim it all because we could lose it any moment," I whisper to myself as I sigh and reach up along the metal racks for a book that doesn't seem to belong there. I frown when I see the title, and then I gasp when I realize it's *The Bridge Across Forever*!

I almost laugh out loud at the coincidence, and I reach back up to the shelf, deciding that I'm gonna leave the book right there.

But suddenly I head a metallic click, and I gasp when I feel the handcuffs close around my wrist, locking me to the metal frame of the bookshelf!

"Bad librarian," comes Brick's voice from behind me, and I gasp again when I turn my head and see that he's wearing nothing but his bulletproof vest and his equipment belt. "You know that it's my job as an officer of the law to punish any government employee who breaks the rules, don't you?"

I'm giggling at the sight of Brick's big cock half erect behind me, and I know immediately that he's been feeling the same weird melancholy that's been building up over the past year, after our wedding ceremony, the pregnancy, the twins, our promotions . . . all that *normal* stuff! Normal and *wonderful*, yes; but our relationship wasn't born under normal conditions. Brick's my man, and he's sensed what I need, what we both need, what our marriage needs. Now and forever.

"How would you know what the rules are?" I whisper as Brick pulls my business skirt up over my ass and squeezes hard as his cock fills out to full mast. "You're just a meathead cop. A bad cop. A dirty cop."

"How dirty?" growls Brick, and I moan as I feel his face down near my rear, his tongue pushing my satin panties into my crack, his saliva soaking through.

"The dirtiest," I groan. "Filthy."

And then I can't speak, because Brick has ripped my panties down the middle, pulled them off me, and stuffed them right into my mouth. Then he smacks my ass hard, two tight slaps on each buttcheek until my face goes red and I'm snorting through my nose. A moment later he's pulled my rear globes so wide apart I can feel the air swirl around my most secret space, and when he licks my asshole tenderly while rubbing my mound from below hard, I just moan and come all over his hand.

"Good girl," he growls, fingering me deep as I shudder through my orgasm. I feel him coat his hand with my wetness, and I hear him greasing his cock up with my juices.

Soon he's fingering my rear hole, making me relax as I pull at my cuffs, whimper through my gag, smile in the darkness as I know that our lives will never be normal, that the way we met will define the rest of our lives, define us forever.

And so when my husband, the father of my twins, my protector, my savior, my dirty, filthy cop finally takes his finger out and presses his enormous cock-head against my wet hole, pushing himself all the way into me and coming almost immediately, blasting his hot load into places that have never been reached, I just turn my head halfway and nod. I don't say a word, and neither does he. We've never done this before, but he doesn't need to ask.

No, he doesn't need to ask, and I don't need to answer, I think as we hold each other in the silence of the stacks, letting that excitement flow through our panting bodies as a reminder of where we've been. And then, when we sneak down the back staircase and make our way to my private office, gaze upon our sleeping babies, I think of where we're going. Going together. As a family.

"What are you doing?" I whisper as Brick reaches into the rockers and picks up our twins, one in each hand, nestling them against his big chest. "Don't wake them!"

But the twins just curl their little fists and nuzzle into Daddy, and I do it too, feeling Brick shudder as he holds his family like the protector he is.

That's who he is. This is who I am. And this was always our story. Just ours.

Always ours.

Forever ours.

∞

FROM THE AUTHOR

OMG, over-the-top to the point of madness,
I know. But fun, I hope? That's the point of
the CURVY FOR HIM series. Just ridiculously hot,
insane stories that obviously would never happen
anywhere except in our little world of silliness and
romantic make-believe.

Looking for something a bit deeper and more complex? Well, try my full-length series CURVES FOR
SHEIKHS and CURVES FOR SHIFTERS.

Thanks for joining us on this wild ride. I understand if my stuff is too out there for you, but I do
hope you stick around.

Love,
Anna.
mail@annabellewinters.com

PS: If you do decide to stick around, join my private
list at **ANNABELLEWINTERS.COM/JOIN** and you'll
get five super-hot epilogues from my SHEIKHS
series.

∞